Lilies
for
Daisy

Jakob Becker

Jakob Becker

DEDICATION

For Olivia

*It's not my heart or soul,
But I'll be damned if it doesn't feel like it.*

Jakob Becker

FOREWORD

Normally at this point you're supposed to put a thing here. Usually that thing is written by someone other than the author as a bit of a "hey look this book doesn't suck because I said so!" sort of deal. However, you would be surprised (sarcasm) how hard it is for a 17 year old with no qualifications to find someone to write a foreword or introduction for them (on account of the fact that they think it'll suck). So here I am, writing my own introduction. So symbolic of my life.

Lilies for Daisy is a story that I started my sophomore year of high school because I had nothing else better to do. It was just a little thing I wrote for fun as a way to decompress after class (or more often than not during). In the beginning, I didn't really plan on publishing it, or really even finishing it for that matter. I mean, why would I? It was just an inside joke with a few friends at the time anyways, so it seemed perfectly logical to just keep writing the stupid thing for fun.

But eventually I changed my mind (about halfway through the first draft), and I decided that I was going to publish it for the memes. So I cleaned it up a bit for the sake of the public eye, killed off a few nonsensical inside jokes that would send my friends and me to the looney bin, and mainly tried to make it sound coherent.

But in my junior year the project evolved into therapy. After a particularly tough part of my life (that for the sake of your time I won't go into) I wrote my pain into the story in an attempt to push it off myself. I'm not sure if it worked, but my own thoughts on life are pretty evident in the story's text. You don't even need to have paid much attention in English class to be able to see it.

So here I am, about a quarter through senior year and applying to colleges, and I published a book. Maybe that's just the kicker I need to get accepted to my top picks, maybe not. I don't care. I'm just impressed that I managed to even get this far.

That's all for this introduction/foreword/author's note.

Hopefully for novel number two I'll actually manage to get someone else to do this because I have no idea what I'm doing, just like everything else in my life.

Lilies for Daisy

LIST OF NOTABLE CONTRIBUTORS

Major Dennis Ammann, Che Baniadam, Jaclyn "Frost" Becker, Jeffrey Becker, Lisa Becker, Ruthlee "Nana" Becker, Lily Bolig, Mary Lee "Grandma" Bowman†, Kathleen Brown, Tessora Bustillos, Doctor Rochelle Calvert, Ryan Cardenas, Cadet Senior Master Sergeant Alexander Davenport, First Lieutenant Jennifer Davenport, Cadet Airman First Class Maximus Davenport, Ellen di Christina, Madelyn Flores, Shayna Glazer, Olivia Hussey, Gaetano Irrera, Benjamin "Aris" Lazerson, Oly Norris, Bill Pohlman, Robert Ross, Alex Shankhuizen, Elyse Simons, Steve Simons, George Stimson, Michael Vickery, Doctor Todd Young

PROLOGUE - I PROMISED I'D BRING YOU FLOWERS

My Sweet Daisy,

Do you remember the promise I made you when we were kids? I said that you'd never have to be alone again, that I'd always be right next to you to take on whatever hardships this life threw at us. I promised I'd never leave the spot reserved for me in your heart, no matter how far away we were from each other. I would be by your side, forever and always.

My lovely Daisy, do you remember that night during the summer? The night I cried for hours in your arms, fearing that you'd be left alone in this world? The two of us sitting on the couch with the television's faint glow in the background and the fireplace warming that tiny house, I confessed my deepest fears to you. Your sweet voice and warm heart washed away whatever terror had engulfed me, and that's where I promised I'd bring you flowers. Upon my homecoming, I'd bring you the most beautiful bouquet of roses I could find, just to show them what a true beauty looks like.

My gorgeous Daisy, do you remember that last kiss? Before I stepped away and took my post among a hundred young men off to save the world, we shared the most deep and passionate kiss. That was the most amazing kiss I'd ever had. I thank the Good Lord that our final goodbyes were so special. And while you were still in my arms, I whispered that promise in your ear. That promise that I would come home with a bouquet of roses, and hours of stories. I'd never have leave your side again.

If you're reading this, then I broke those promises. That kiss will be the last one we'll ever share. These stories of my adventures shall go untold, forgotten and lost in the sea of green uniforms and white stars. My place at your side will go unfilled, at least for a while. But, even through this lamented barrier, I know someone brought you those flowers. Maybe they weren't the red roses of love and passion, but I know they made it to your doorstep... somehow.

Daisy, the entire time I was out in this dusty wasteland, I never once stopped thinking about you. The thought of your smile, your laugh, your everything... that's what got me through every tiny bit of pain this desert inflicted upon me. No matter how terrible things were, I knew why I was out here, what I was fighting to protect: you.

It was never about America, or the flag, or the American people. It was always about you. There truly is no greater honor than fighting for, and dying for, the people I love the most.

Don't cry for me, Daisy. I may be gone, but I haven't left your side. I exist within your heart and mind, where I shall forever rest. Even in death, I shall forever remain the one thing in this world I ever wanted to be:

Yours.

CHAPTER 1 - ULYSSES

It wasn't a secret to anyone that Harvard absolutely hated his job. He oriented the trifold American flag sitting on the desk so that it could be in the most aesthetically pleasing position as possible. Each pile of papers was sorted through carefully, the unimportant documents being shredded and tossed whilst anything spared was alphabetized. On the floor in the immaculate cubicle was a gray plastic trashcan sitting solitarily in the corner.

The cubicle itself was nothing special. It was constructed from standard gray partitions which held photographs and memorabilia from the lieutenant's civilian life. The desk itself was made of the composite imitation wood found in almost every American classroom, however this particular one had been scrubbed down and buffed so that Harvard could barely see his reflection in it's surface. Some sort of potted shrub sat motionless in the corner of the desk's workspace. It was a fair shade of green with only a few visible brown spots from malnourishment and a forgetful caretaker. Thankfully, Harvard always remembered to water the poor shrub, which had been given the name "Phillip" for no reason at all.

However, one particular part of this cubicle always caught Harvard's attention, and that was the wooden crucifix that hung on the wall above the Lieutenant's outdated laptop. It was beautiful, being carved of fine mahogany and beveled so that it seemed to be popping out at him. The florescent lights on the ceiling reflected off it's glassy surface, and somehow was always devoid of dust and blemishes even if Harvard never touched it before. It was disgusting.

With a last quick wipe down of the lieutenant's grime covered keyboard, Harvard slumped in the bureau's chair. He sighed in accomplishment having finished his one task for the day: organize First Lieutenant Paul's desk. It was a peculiar task for Harvard's particular career as an army infantryman, as he worked mainly as Paul's personal secretary and general slave. This being said, he really didn't mind at all. It was either organizing desks, doing coffee runs, following Paul around like a babysitter, or doing actual work with Second Lieutenant Stern's platoon; a fate worse than death in the eyes of many.

He ran his fingers along the seams of the cushions, gently rotating the chair clockwise for a bit, then reversing the direction and rotated counterclockwise, then changed his direction once more. Harvard repeated this oscillation for a little while, his back to the rest of the offices when he heard a voice behind him. "Howdy sir." The voice obviously belonged to a younger man, and most definitely a new recruit.

Harvard oriented the chair to face the source of the voice, where his suspicions were confirmed. The soldier was in the full Army Combat Uniform with a spotless pair of tan service boots to go with it. On his sternum, there was a fuzzy square where the rank insignia was supposed to go, however it appeared that this private had not yet attained a real rank. He was what the men referred to as "a fuzzy". The private's near black hair was cut to regulation, he was clean shaved although tiny specks of black stubble dotted a chiseled chin. Harvard realized this private was quite good looking. A sharp jawline squared off his face, his light brown eyes seemed to have gold dust embedded into them that sparkled in the florescent lights, but perhaps his best feature was his smile. It was the kind of grin that could melt a woman's heart, the kind of smile that made a man trust him. It was truly the smile of a good old Texas boy. Harvard already hated him.

"What do you want, private…" He paused as his eyes met the fuzzy rectangle that a nametape was supposed to be attached to. "Um… what's your name?"

The private never lost that impeccable grin, even as he talked, "My name's Carl. Nice to meet you, sir." Harvard cringed at the sound of his voice. Not only was the private good looking, but he had a southern accent to go with his heart stopping features. Even his voice embodied the trustworthy southern politician attitude.

"No, no, no. We go by last names here. I'm Harvard, but my first name is Reginald. What's your last name?" Harvard, at least to himself, sounded reminiscent of a teenager who's voice only halfway developed during puberty. It wasn't a flute by any means, but it wasn't the bellowing and gruff soldier's voice.

"Oh… my last name is Darling." Silence filled the room.

"Okay Carl, why are you here?" Harvard finally asked after an awkward minute of silence. Carl's cheerful attitude returned in full swing.

"Well sir, I was told by Master Sergeant Abram to report here to pick up the Humvee keys." Harvard laughed almost uncontrollably with memories of his first day flooding back. Poor Carl had no idea that Abram had sent him on a snipe quest.

Eventually he managed to calm himself. "Okay, okay… Give me a moment." He inhaled deeply, then let out a long winded exhale, "So, I'm not the lieutenant. I'm a Private First Class. And Humvee keys don't exist… and Abram's kind of a dick." Carl chuckled.

"Ah I figured as much. So are you assigned to Miserable Company too?"

"Yeah, and it looks like we're both in Alpha Platoon as well. First squad?"

"Yep."

"Then we're in the same squad too." Harvard forced a smile, figuring that he'd actually have to be nice to the private since they'll be in such close proximity to each other. "Alright, well why don't you take a seat and we'll get to know each other a bit."

Carl's eyes fell upon a metal folding chair that sat on the side of the cubicle's desk. It was rusted at the hinges, and a sickly gray color like the cubicle partitions. The pegs at the bottoms had yellowed with age, the rubber cracked and flaking. Carl still sat in it without any complaint, a closed mouth smile still on his face.

Harvard began tapping his fingers on the desk, thinking of something to ask his new squad mate. Carl broke the silence first, "So, Harvard, how long have you been out here?"

"Somewhere around six months. And this is your first day I take it?" Carl nodded, "How are you liking it so far?"

His eyes scanned the office, taking in every detail he possibly could. "It's alright I guess. As far as deployments go, I could've gone somewhere real bad like Iraq or Syria."

"Yep. Welcome to Birkinistan, the only place in the entire world where normal military procedures were thrown out the window a long time ago, and the whole place runs like insanity. But it seems to be working."

A loud rumbling sound propagated from Carl's belly, causing both him and Harvard to giggle. "Hungry?"

"Yep."

"Don't worry pal…" Harvard furrowed his eyebrow as the realization hit him that he had fallen under Carl's spell. Nevertheless he continued his statement, "Chow's at 18:00, and it's 17:43 right now. Just a few more minutes." Harvard studied Carl's features once more and thought that perhaps this private really was just a good old country boy. Or maybe he was secretly a racist who lynches black people on the weekends.

"Ah I can't wait. What's on the menu tonight?" Carl asked.

"Well, tonight's Taco Tuesday. The cooks here are pretty good too." Harvard paused, "Well, not Air Force and Navy good, but better than the Marines and other Army bases." Carl simply nodded in response as the rumbling of a fighter jet taking off rattled the offices. The disgusting gray carpeted floors rattled, the white painted wooden walls shook, casting ever so minuscule bits of chipped paint into the air.

"I like tacos." Carl declared, prompting a chuckle from Harvard.

"I do too." He added. From seemingly out of nowhere, a third individual entered the cubicle space. He was just above average height with non regulation blonde hair that was messy and covered in a fine layer of sweat from being under a cover. His irises were almost red, like a glass of wine illuminated by candlelight. His skin was once pale as a sheet of printer paper, but months on end spent in the Birkinistani desert had tanned him to the point of looking more like someone of oriental descent. A short nose punctuated his features being perfectly centered in his face. He wore the exact same uniform as both Carl and Harvard, say for the single black rectangle on his sternum.

In an instant, Carl stood up from his seat and greeted First Lieutenant Paul with a "Howdy sir." Paul cringed, then focused his attention on Harvard, who was slumped back in the chair without a care in the world.

"At least this one greeted me, Private." Paul did his best to sound intimidating, but failed miserably by breaking bearing with a smile.

"How long have you known me?" Harvard smiled in an attempt to replicate Carl's impeccable grin.

"Too long..." Paul sighed and examined Harvard's handiwork for a few moments, then pointed backwards with his thumb as an order for him to get out of his seat. Reluctantly, Harvard complied and stood next to Carl.

The lieutenant flopped into his chair and folded his hands together as he inspected Harvard's work more carefully. Eventually he addressed Carl, "So, are you Carl... Darling?" He asked.

"Yes sir!" Carl replied with great enthusiasm. Paul shifted his attention to Harvard.

"Where do you find these guys?"

"Dude, I have no idea."

"Okay Darling... I refuse to call you that. Carl, welcome to the 159th Infantry Division, 1st Brigade, 4th Battalion, Miserable Company, Alpha Platoon, First Squad. I am your platoon commander, First Lieutenant Jimmy Paul. Your platoon sergeant is Master Sergeant Donovan Abram. Private First Class Reginald

Harvard here, is your squad leader. Sort of, I mean Alpha Platoon is so weird." Paul sighed and tapped his foot on the floor to an imaginary beat.

"How weird, sir?" Carl asked.

"Harvard?"

"Like normal army weird, Birkinistan standard. This place makes no sense, ever... I mean, *ever*." Carl nodded and grunted in understanding.

In a moment of silence, Harvard checked his watch to find the time was 17:52. "Hey, I'm heading off to the chow-hall. I'll be at the normal place." His choice of words caused Paul to groan in displeasure.

"Harvard, please for the love of God call it the DFAC, you sound like an old man." He slumped back in his chair, and propped his feet up on his desk.

"De-fuck?" Carl's voice was almost childlike, "How does one de-fuck themselves?" He tilted his head like a confused dog.

"It's Dee-FACK, short for dining facility. Don't worry about the jargon, everyone gets used to it at some point." Harvard's eyes fell upon the lieutenant, "Am I free to go, sir?"

"Get out of here, your archaic vocabulary is making me sick." He laughed, "I'm going to get Carl situated, go over some of our... traditions. I'll take him over when I'm done, good?"

"Good. See ya then." Harvard tipped an imaginary hat on his head, then began walking out of the cube farm. Being this late into the evening, the offices weren't as busy as they normally were. Many of the cubicles sat in disorganization, papers strewn about, trash cans hadn't been emptied in days. The only two cubicles that were respectable were Paul's and the revered Second Lieutenant Stern's.

He flung the doors of the offices open and walked out onto the airfield. The building was situated on a concrete slab next to a chain link fence that separated the runway from the administrative buildings. The runway itself was black asphalt and just over half a mile in length, punctuated by white lines and strings of lights that flashed parallel with the edges. A tall and menacing air traffic control tower sat on the opposite side of the runway from the administration buildings, a radar dish spinning ominously atop the tower. It was essentially a concrete monolith that was filled with the least competent air traffic control unit in the history of military aviation.

A warm breeze of desert air wafted the faint scent of gasoline towards him. Even with the sun slowly dipping behind the mountains surrounding the airfield, the desert heat never fully dissipated.

A rumbling sensation in Harvard's stomach reminded him that he was in need of sustenance, or as the normal people call it, hungry. So with a step off with his left foot, he began half-walking-half-marching towards the DFAC. Each footfall was punctuated by a dull click of hard rubber on concrete, filling Harvard with an odd sense of satisfaction. He had always enjoyed the sound of pristine military style boots on concrete, as the noise was unique to that class of footwear. Even during his civilian life he would often wear combat boots just so he could create that wonderful sound.

He stopped at the entrance of the DFAC, taking a brief moment to admire the faint scent of the kitchen escaping through ventilation shafts. Harvard simply couldn't wait any longer. He firmly pulled the metal handles on the doors, then swiftly made his way inside.

That's when the aroma of freshly prepared Mexican style ground beef, fried tortillas, and Santa Fe style rice invaded Harvard's nose like a tidal wave. The delicious smells were so strong and prominent, Harvard could taste the food before it had so much as met his gaze.

He plopped a standard plastic tray and plate on the slide counter, then reached into a bucket full of plastic silverware to obtain the necessary equipment for his mission: food time. He slid his tray down to the first available server, who asked in a rather annoyed tone, "Beef or chicken?"

"Beef." Harvard replied equally as cold. The server scooped a wad of ground beef into a taco shell, sprinkled some lettuce and cheese, then placed it on Harvard's plate. She repeated this process once more to manufacture a second taco.

"Anything else?" She asked, her voice hoarse from probably a long deployment in the desert. One look at her rank insignia, being only two chevrons, meant that she probably had been out here for quite some time.

"No, thank you." He continued along his path, grabbing a foam container of refried beans from under a heat lamp, then a box of apple juice from an ice bucket in the counter. He neatly arranged everything on his tray so that it was aesthetically pleasing and nothing fell off, then maneuvered through the DFAC which had progressively become more crowded.

First Squad plus Paul and Abram's normal spot was in the furthermost side of the DFAC from the slide counter, and right next to the latrines. There was nothing notable about the spot, having the same polyurethane tables that had been scratched from years of soldiers eating there. It was large enough to seat a squad of 12, but

First Squad was only made up of six soldiers counting Paul and Abram.

Harvard picked his normal seat, and waited without even touching his steaming, fresh, delicious tacos. He was better than that, and always waited for his friends to show up before he began his meal. Thankfully, he didn't need to wait too long as the first of his friends sat down: Specialist Gerolf Herbert. "Hey." The almost white haired soldier greeted Harvard without so much as making eye contact. Herbert was average in height, width, build, and looks. The only non average thing about Herbert, at least to Harvard's speculation, his small penis. Harvard never bothered to confirm his suspicions, but it would only make sense.

"Hey Herbert." Harvard replied unenthusiastically. The Specialist sat directly across from Harvard and began unpacking his package of sweetcorn. Herbert wasn't nearly as polite as Harvard, and began eating almost immediately. Watching him eat caused Harvard's stomach to rumble.

The second to arrive was Private Murray Fern, who carried an absurd amount of food. His scruffy brown hair was completely out of regulation, his face was covered in thin fibers of beard hair probably from not shaving in a week. His uniform was atrocious, sporting what Harvard could only assume was pizza sauce stains and more wrinkles than a 90 year old man. But perhaps the most atrocious part of Fern was the constant stench of incense or industrial grade air freshener that radiated off of him like an aura.

Fern placed his mountain of food on the table which made an audible thump. His tray was stacked with five tacos—three beef and two chicken—a bowl of beans, a bowl of rice, and to top it all off, an extra large plastic cup of cola. It was amazing that Fern was even in weight standards, and even more amazing that he didn't look obese in the slightest.

"How did you even pass basic?" Herbert asked as the scruffy man began opening his assorted dishes. In response, all Fern did was giggle. He attempted to take a gulp from his cola, but failed to swallow from a giggle escaping his lips. The two made eye contact, with Herbert just glaring at the private and Fern trying his hardest not to bust out laughing.

The last of the punctual crew sat down, being the revered platoon sergeant: Master Sergeant Donovan Abram. He was so muscular he looked like he was a bag of rocks covered in flesh. His head was completely bald and so shiny Harvard assumed he polished it. But perhaps his most striking feature was his set of icy blue eyes that sent a shiver down any man's spine. He sat down next to Herbert, who greeted him with the standard "Good evening, sergeant." Abram gave no response.

Abram's tray was nonexistent, as he opted to bring a standard issue MRE instead. He grunted as he ripped the package open with his teeth, then dumped the contents onto the table.

"Abram, why don't you ever eat normal people food?" Harvard asked.

"R'minds me a 'Nam." He replied in the most hoarse and gruff voice possible.

"You're 36." Harvard reminded him.

"I can dream!" The Master Sergeant barked as be propped his flameless ration heater against a rock or something. Since everyone who was normally on time was seated, Harvard picked up his first taco and took a bite out of it. They smelled much better than they tasted. The meat was dry and flavorless, the lettuce was soggy, and the corn tortilla shell tasted like cardboard. The only thing about the taco that resembled civilian standards was the cheese, and even that was little bit crunchy. It was the best food Harvard had eaten all week.

Not too much later, Paul had brought Carl to the table. "I'm hoping you've met these folks already." Carl nodded in response. "Good! They're my favorite squad out of all my men... and Stern's. Miserable Company's Alpha Platoon's very own First Squad... and Abram." Abram released a single grunt in acknowledgment. "Gentlemen, this is Private Carl... Carl. Be nice to him, he's a bit... uh... how do you say it?" He trailed off for a moment, "slow?"

"Howdy, folks." He gave the men a charismatic smile and a friendly wave.

"Welcome to Birkinistan, Carl." Herbert returned his smile with one of his own. Harvard recognized that smile though, and immediately felt a bit of remorse for the poor kid. He locked eyes with Herbert and shook his head, though Herbert responded with a simple shrug. He wasn't going to let petty things like morals get in the way of his plans.

Harvard took a few more bites of his taco, then noticed how Fern was eating. He would take a bite of one taco, then shoved some of every side dish in his mouth, take a swig of cola, and then swallow everything with a loud gulp. It repulsed Harvard to the point that he had to avert his eyes to avoid throwing up.

Thankfully, Carl broke the awkward silence which helped distract him a bit. "So, is the base named after Ulysses S. Grant?" Paul shook his head.

"Nope. It's actually named after Odysseus from Homer's epic poem, *The Odyssey*, actually." Paul explained.

"You said 'actually' twice." Herbert smirked.

"Fuck off." Paul took a sip of his water bottle.

"But wait, if Odysseus is Odyssey, how is the Ulysses?" Fern asked.

"What?" Carl giggled.

"He's probably high again." Herbert took a bite of his chicken taco.

"Fern, what the hell are you talking about?" Abram's voice sounded like a mallet on a slab of meat.

"Ulysses is the Latin translation for Odysseus. It's supposed to represent the journey to freedom for Birkinistan, or some bullshit like that." Harvard explained in an attempt to keep the conversation going to prevent Fern from continuing to eat everything at once.

"Thanks Harvard." Paul sipped his water. "So Carl, you know why we're here, right?" Carl nodded.

"Take chemical weapons from the hajis, give the Birkinistani people a structured system of order, then go home." Carl took a bite out of his beef taco.

Paul smiled, his eyes closing ever so slightly as he did. "Awesome! You're already way ahead of most of the privates on their first day."

"And, being a Texan, we can't forget about Arlington." Carl's words echoed in the air as they left his lips.

"Right." Paul sighed. The men slowly returned to their food as the word "Arlington" rang out of existence.

Abram cleared his throat, "Hey, Carl. I'm going to need your help after chow tonight. I got some ID10T forms filled out and Captain Porfiry, he's in charge of the company of MP's here, has them. When you're done with dinner, I'm gonna need you to get them." Even with a clear throat, his voice still sounded like sandpaper.

Carl replied with a that smile of a politician, "Sure thing, Sarge."

"I like your attitude." Abram covered his mouth with his hand to hide a smirk. Harvard's eyes happened to catch Fern sticking the straw of his soda into his container of refried beans, and drink it like a bean smoothie. Harvard shuddered.

Quickly he shifted his eyes to Carl, partially to help him feel welcome in the new unit, but mainly to keep himself from vomiting. "Carl, say, er…" He had lost his train of thought from the refried smoothie, "Um… I got a dog back at the hospital. He's getting his biannual check up… and… stuff. When you're done with Abram, do you want to come with me to pick him up, and like, take him for a walk or something?" He scratched the back of his head.

Carl's eyes seemed to light up with excitement, "Of course! That sounds great, I love dogs!" His enthusiasm was akin to a child being told he was going to a candy store. Harvard wasn't even lying. He really did have a dog at the medical center. "What's his name? Or her's." Carl asked.

"PFC Ranger. Our squad's IED sniffer." Harvard explained. Nobody said a word after that, which forced him to have to listen to Fern slurp his refried beans dishonorably.

Fern opened his mouth to expose all of the macerated food bits. Harvard gagged. "You know what I think?" He asked.

"Nobody gives a shit." Abram growled.

"I think neighbors should neighb, helicopters should helicopt, and raptors should rap…" there was a pause as he stared off into space, "p-p-p-p-pterodactyl!" Everyone slowly turned their gaze to the terrible excuse for a soldier.

"Hey Fern?" Abram asked.

"Yeah?"

"You fucking retard, what the fuck kinda fuckery is this? Did your momma drop you?" Abram lightly smacked him on the back of the head, propelling a tiny chunk of refried beans from his maw. The projectile bean nugget flew across the table and landed in Harvard's left nostril.

Instinctively Harvard inhaled in surprise, which shot the nugget into his nose. He gagged, and coughed, flopping out of his chair and onto the floor. "Harvard?" Carl's voice gave the impression that he was only slightly concerned that his squad leader was dying.

He quickly picked himself off of the floor, and sprinted to the latrines as fast as he could. He flung open the first available stall and practically slid on his knees to the toilet bowl. He hurled a mass of green and brown goo into the white porcelain basin. The caustic stench of vomit crept into Harvard's nostrils forcing more bile to eject from his mouth. A voice emanated from the doorway, "Harvard, you good?" It was Paul, and he was trying his hardest not to laugh.

"I am going to die in this fucking bathroom!" He managed to shout, but the force exerted on his throat caused him to hurl some more. His breathing accelerated from panic to hyperventilation from the vomit stopping his breathing.

"You sure? We can get a doctor." It was a second voice. The Texan with the perfect face and stupidly charming smile.

"Shut the fuck up Carl!" He half-cried-half-screamed, thanking a God he didn't believe in that his heaving had ceased.

"I'll get a doc if you need one!" Paul shouted. Harvard grasped tighter on the toilet basin thinking to himself that if his friends really cared, they'd come in and check on him themselves.

"Go fuck yourselves!"

"Love you too, buddy no homo!" Paul chuckled. The sound of two pairs of boots slowly marching away told Harvard that his commander and squad mate had left him to puke his organs out. He was in no real state to care. He just sat on the floor of the stall, breathing heavily, as he flopped his hand on the metal toilet handle. The toilet whirled and screamed as the water washed away Harvard's mess, soon it appeared as if nothing had happened at all except for the lingering stench.

He slowly picked himself up from off the floor in a bit of a daze. With a groan, Harvard dusted off his trousers as he staggered to the sinks to tidy himself up a bit. One look in the mirror told him that simply washing his hands and face was not going to make him any more presentable. Light brown hair that had been somewhat groomed earlier that day was a scruffy mess that resembled more of a frilled paint brush. Though he wasn't particularly bad looking, he was just sort of average. The sweat that had accumulated on his face from the ordeal highlighted his acne scars from his teenage years in the florescent lights, as well as the easily visible slash scar across his left cheek. The whites of his eyes were bloodshot and moist, presumably from the pungent odors of his vomit. "Fuck it." He muttered as he splashed some water on his face, "I ain't trying to impress anybody."

The moment he turned to walk out of the latrines, he felt bile rise to his throat again. In a panicked flurry of motion, he resumed his post at the toilet basin heaving his dinner out of his body.

CHAPTER 2 - RANGER

A few hours had passed since the war crimes had been committed in the DFAC. Harvard had just finished cleaning himself up in the shower trailer and had changed into a completely new uniform, minus the boots. When he had exited the pitiful excuse for a bathhouse, he found his lieutenant standing outside tapping his foot in rapid succession. The moment their gazes met, his eyes lit up. "Harvard!" He exclaimed, panic evident in his voice, "So, uh… have you read the newspaper lately?"

Harvard grumbled, "No I'm not an old man."

"Radio? TV? Wait, do you guys even get cable?" He asked.

"No. We're given a satellite phone to call our families and that's it." The private furrowed his eyebrows before asking, "Do they give *you* cable?"

"That's not important…" Paul paused, "Yes." Harvard groaned and rolled his eyes, "Look, that's not the point. Did you hear about what happened in the Southern Province just a few hours ago?"

Harvard leaned against the wall of the shower trailer, "No. Fill me in."

"Birks gassed half a city. Hundreds KIA, hundreds more injured." Harvard felt a shiver run down his entire body. "Mainly civilian casualties. The United Nations is calling for another emergency Security Council meeting." His heart sank.

For the next few moments, neither of the men said a word. They simply stood in the desert twilight while the world marched on without them. At last, Harvard spoke, "Arlington all over again."

Paul's only reply was a somber, "Yeah." The silence returned, but only briefly. Paul titled his head in a gesture to prompt Harvard to follow him. They walked side by side, boots crunching the gravel underfoot to produce a soft and melodic sound familiar to every man who lived on base.

"So they really don't give you cable?" Paul was perplexed.

"No."

"What do you do for fun then?"

"Oh, y'know… set up cans on the steps at the CHU and try to knock them down by tossing pebbles at them, read a bit, play Texas Hold'em. Think of insults more creative than 'sand niggers'. Normal stuff." Harvard shifted his gaze to his lieutenant, "They give you cable?"

"Yeah in the break room we've got a latte machine, fridge, and a 4k TV with cable."

"Seriously?"

"Yeah." Paul sucked his bottom lip into his mouth and scrunched his brows together, "Wait, why are we here?" They stopped in front of the base's hospital, a squatty repurposed factory from the Cold War. The entire thing had been refitted with modern medical appliances and was on par with many civilian hospitals in the States.

Harvard exhaled sharply, "Do you even pay attention? Ranger. Checkup. Ring any bells?"

"Honestly half the time I just tune you guys out." Paul smiled innocently.

"Well at least you're honest." Harvard firmly pulled on the industrial doors to the entrance and held it open for his commander before following him inside. To his surprise, he found Carl and Ranger both sound asleep. Carl had propped himself up against the wall while seated in a metal folding chair; the dog snored quietly at his feet. "I have a feeling they'll be good friends." Harvard said with a smile.

"How so?" Paul began walking up to the front desk to see if anyone was around for checkout.

"They've got relatively the same IQ." He paused, "Actually that might be an insult to the dog."

Paul chuckled, "That's not funny."

"It's a little funny." Ranger picked his head up from off the floor at the sound of his owner's voice. The moment their eyes met, the dog stood up with a yawn and groggily walked up to Harvard. He sniffed his boot, then collapsed onto the floor trapping both of Harvard's feet underneath him.

He reached down to scratch his dog's back, allowing fur to shed and float around the lobby like little fairies. Ranger didn't react to his owner scratching his back lovingly and instead passed out at his feet.

Carl stirred a moment before rubbing sleep from his eyes. He scanned the room briefly, then smiled as he recognized Harvard. "He's such a good boy." Ranger wagged his tail a single time, "I got him checked out and everything. Doc says he's all set, nothing to report. Vaccines all taken care of, blood tests done, and all that." Paul stopped looking for a way to summon the receptionist and leaned against the desk. "Oh, and Harvard, by the way, did you know that Abram is mean?"

Instantly both he and Paul started laughing, "Trust me man, I've been living with that guy for the past six months. I'm quite aware." Harvard glanced to Paul to see if he had anything to add, but instead found that he was just smiling like an idiot. "So I guess you learned that ID10T forms don't exist."

"Yeah. Captain Porfiry, he's really nice by the way, wrote it out for me on a piece of paper and it spelled out 'idiot'!" Carl stood up from his seat and stretched, "Does Abram think I'm an idiot?"

Before Harvard could open his mouth to say, "I think you're an idiot," Paul said, "I don't think he thinks you're smart. You just need to prove to him you are." Harvard rolled his eyes, then focused his attention to Ranger who was back in a deep sleep. "Hey, how long were you waiting for us?" The lieutenant asked.

Carl furrowed his brow, "I think it was only ten, fifteen minutes. I'm just pretty jet lagged I guess." He smiled that impeccable and despicable smile. Harvard really wanted to punch him in the mouth.

"Well, sir. I believe it's bed time." Harvard yawned.

"Agreed, my friend. Goodnight Carl! We've got a big day tomorrow." Harvard squirmed. "Big day" usually meant long marches in the desert sun. With that, however, the private first class and the first lieutenant began walking away with Ranger slowly following behind.

"Oh, uh, wait. Harvard?" Carl's innocent and childlike voice forced Harvard to press his lips together and form fists with his hands.

"Yes? Carl?" He croaked.

"Do you know where C-H-U S-59 is?" Harvard glared at his lieutenant who was just smiling innocently.

"Why?" He mouthed to his superior. He cleared his throat, "It's pronounced 'CHOO' as in, I chew my food." He sighed, "That's my—excuse me—*our* house. I guess you'll be living there too."

Paul whispered, "Sorry," to his soldier who returned this with an extension of his middle finger. "I hope you don't snore!" Harvard now wanted to punch Paul in the mouth.

"Nah. Not since basic." Harvard was going to kill him. With that, the three plus Ranger began walking towards the plot of land filled with CHUs, apply named "CHUville". It was essentially a massive empty field filled with repurposed shipping containers that housed soldiers. Some of these "Containerized Housing Units" were outfitted with showers, but most of them weren't. Most of them—say for the unlucky few—had a working AC unit.

S-59 was the second closest to the runway on S-Block, and was one of the many units that wasn't outfitted with a shower. It was slightly larger than the others on base, with enough room to comfortably house four men and their gear. This extra space was left largely unused as only Harvard and Paul lived there with the dog. The extra bunks were used as storage to keep the men's stuff off the floor.

Harvard pushed the door open and held it for the others. The men piled in and flipped on the light casting a pale glow upon the immaculate living quarters. Everything was neatly packed in duffle bags that sat on the top bunks. All of their earthly possessions were in those bags—clothes, books, equipment, and other personal items.

Paul fell face first into his bed and passed out right there without so much as taking off his boots. Harvard shook his head. "Well, here it is. Home sweet home." He shifted his gaze to the private to watch him examine the room. It truly was just a shipping container with bunk beds in it, but it was home to them. At least, it was as close to home as things got in Birkinistan.

"Which bunk is mine?" Carl asked. Harvard pointed to the bunk that was above the bed Paul had flopped in.

"We'll clear the stuff up there and move it under the bed and wherever else we can get it out of the way. The bed's unkept, but that's okay. We can make it in the morning… or not. Not like anyone inspects us." He yawned.

"That's kind of out of character, Harv. I'd expect you to want to keep this place spotless." Carl tilted his head to the side.

"Nah, I just like keeping things out of the way in here." He yawned with more vigor, "Just, move your shit. I need a nap." He stumbled to his bunk and sat down on the mattress. All he did was watch Carl move Paul's belongings off his bed without lifting a finger to help. After all, it wasn't his job to assist in bed making operations.

A laundry bag fell from the heavens and onto the linoleum floors with a muffled thump as the air inside was forced out. Then came a duffle bag full of assorted articles of clothing and other belongings that impacted the floor with a much more pronounced thud. "Did it." Carl announced

"Awesome. This is where you'll be sleeping for the next… however long you're stuck here." Harvard smiled. "Now, we have a rule here. No one sleeps naked… except for the dog. If you must sleep in minimal clothing, sleep in your undies. Otherwise, PT shorts and shirt will double as pajamas." He shuddered as flashbacks from basic training entered his thoughts. "Nobody... sleeps... naked..." He repeated, mainly for himself.

Carl chuckled a bit, "Don't worry about that." He gave Harvard a warm smile, "Thanks for making me feel welcomed today. It's much appreciated."

He couldn't help but smile back, "Yeah, no problem. I was new too once, I get it." With that, Carl unzipped his boots and neatly set them down next to Paul's. Then he unbuttoned his blouse and draped it over the side of his bunk.

Harvard too began getting ready for bed. He unzipped his boots and let them hit the floor with a satisfying thump. He swung his legs up and laid himself flat on his bed, his head resting on his pillow.

Ranger jumped on top of the bed as well, resting his head on Harvard's chest. He scratched behind the dog's ears, causing him to snort and surrender to his owner's affection. He touched Harvard's nose with his tongue, causing a small smile to form on his face.

With a click, the CHU was submerged in darkness. The faint metallic clicking of feet ascending the metal ladder was the only thing that disturbed the stillness. There was an all but silent rustling of fabric as Carl made himself comfortable in his bed. "G'night, Harvard."

"Night, Carl." With that, silence filled the room. Harvard was quite comfortable with his dog laying on him. He felt at peace enough to shut his eyes. Eventually, exhaustion overtook him as he drifted off into dreamland.

~ ~ ~

The night passed, darkness shrouded the airfield as many of the lights slowly flipped off. Small blue, green, red, and white lights dotted the runway in preparation for planes that wouldn't land anytime soon. In the cloudless skies above sat a full pale moon, casting a cool white glow upon the black desert. Winds blew through the airfield, coming in from the east, whistling the songs of the desert night through the cracks in the doorframe.

At 04:58, Harvard awoke. He didn't lift his head off his pillow, nor did he even open his eyes. All he did was run his fingers through Ranger's fur, listening to his faint, rhythmic breathing. Eventually, he did open his eyes to look around the room. Carl and Paul were sound asleep, their quiet breathing barely audible in the silent room.

Harvard lifted his head off his pillow, much to the dismay of the sleeping Ranger. The dog quietly groaned in protest as his owner moved his legs out from under the covers. Slowly, he found himself climbing out of bed, his sock covered feet meeting the frigid linoleum.

Since he was already this far gone from falling back asleep, he decided it was time to do some morning physical training. He slipped his feet into a pair of running shoes that were strategically placed facing away from his bed. They were the kind that didn't have laces, which made them incredibly easy to put on in his early morning braindead state.

Quietly, he crept out of the CHU, taking great care not to disturb the others. Each footfall was as light as could be, making only a faint tap that was quieter than a pin drop. He twisted the door handle as gently as he could, then pushed the door open just wide enough so he could sneak out into the crisp morning air.

The differences in temperature from five in the morning to six always astonished Harvard. It was 55 degrees Fahrenheit now, but in only an hour the sun would poke it's head out from behind the mountains and the concrete would become hot enough to scramble an egg. Due to the sudden heat difference, the early morning hours were the best time to get some exercise in—not that anyone on base was ever inclined to do so.

He gently shut the door, twisting the handle to reduce the noise. Once he was sure the outside world would no longer disturb his sleeping roommates, he inhaled deeply through his nose, wafting in the scents of diesel and grease. The crispness of the air stung his nostrils, yet it still felt refreshing. The tops of the mountains were painted a deep orange as the sun began its daily ascension, while the skies above still embraced the deep blues and purples of midnight.

With a closed smile on his face, he began walking along the gravel pathway to the edge of the runway. He was interrupted by the sound of a CHU door closing on his left. He turned his head to find a man dressed in pristine ACUs. At his sternum there was a gold colored vertical rectangle, a Second Lieutenant, one rank below Paul. Harvard glanced at this lieutenant's nametape, which read "Stern". "Ah crap." He muttered.

Second Lieutenant Stern put his hands on his hips and glared at Harvard before asking, "You blind? Can you not see my rank? I'm warranted a salute, y'know." This was the revered commander of Miserable Company's Bravo Platoon—a slightly taller than average man with out of regulation black hair, stubble encrusted face covered in acne scars from his youth. His piercing blue eyes matched Abram's for intimidation, but the rest of Stern's scrawny body and arrogant manners destroyed any authoritative respect he might have gotten. "If you keep standing there I might just have to report you to your commander."

Harvard didn't say a word. Instead, he snapped to the position of attention, raised his bladed hand up his gig line, then planted it firmly in his pocket. It was no secret that Harvard, just like everyone else, had zero respect for him.

In response, the second lieutenant simply scoffed while shaking his head before walking away towards the offices. Harvard rolled his eyes and continued until he found himself at the runway's edge.

He began jogging at a light pace, listening to the sound of his feet thumping against the tarmac. He allowed his mind to wander when he was training, as he found nothing else better to do. The scenery around him was nothing special, just a dark airfield with CHUs, hangers and other facilities on each side.

Through the thumps of his feet on the tarmac, Harvard heard the faint booming of what he thought was a motorcycle through the cracks in the mountainside. It sounded very far away, so he didn't pay it much mind. He was lost in the rhythmic sounds of his feet on the runway—the drums to an imaginary silent melody.

He rounded one of the four corners on his jog, when it occurred to him that the sound of the motorcycle hadn't gone away. In fact, he thought it was louder than before. He slowed his pace progressively until he came to a halt to listen to the sound.

With the sound of his footfalls no longer clouding his hearing, he came to the realization that the source of the sound wasn't a motorcycle at all. It was the familiar repeating dull cracks of helicopter blades slicing air. This realization caused his hairs to stand on edge—helicopters weren't supposed to be flying around at this time, at least not to or out of Ulysses. He rationalized this by presuming that it was perhaps a bird from a forward operating base.

He began jogging again, although he didn't get too far before the air raid sirens on base screeched, sending a wave of heat through his entire body. Immediately soldiers from all corners of the base rushed out of their CHUs or stations to get to cover or arm themselves to fend off the incoming attack.

Harvard, in all of his bravery, felt his heart fly into his throat as he sprinted into the nearest hanger. This particular one housed an M2A2 Bradley—an armored vehicle used by the cavalry scouts. He plopped himself on the ground, using the side armor of the Bradley as lumbar support while he calmed his nerves.

The world seemed as though it wouldn't let Harvard rest for even a moment. Just as soon as he began to calm down, the Bradley roared to life, causing him to lurch forward in a flurry of motion and cacophony of screams. Two soldiers had watched the entire spectacle, and where giggling quietly in the corner of the hanger. He dusted himself off glaring at the two with fire in his eyes. He stopped, however, once his eyes met the girl's. Pale skin, short red hair, such a nice body and—his thoughts were immediately interrupted by the sudden echoing of rifle fire resonating off the mountains surrounding the base.

Harvard quickly turned his head to face the runway, where he saw an impromptu battery of anti-aircraft weapons systems which included a few M1A1 Abrams, two M2A2 Bradleys which the one from the hanger soon joined with, and even a soldier wearing nothing but his boxers and a tactical vest wielding a Javelin guided missile system.

He walked outside to see the mountains where the helicopter would poke its head out only to be slaughtered the mass of anti aircraft materiel at the ready. He knew he was in very little danger; if the helicopter were to target anyone it would probably be the anti-air battery plus shirtless guy.

The helicopter finally appeared from behind the hills with thick black smoke spewing from it's engines. Even from the easily three kilometer distance, it was clear as day that the hull was riddled in bullets. With all of the markings on the exterior pretty much erased, it was near impossible to tell who the craft belonged to.

That being the case, the bird was an Mi-8 gunship that appeared to be one of the later Soviet models. Since the United States didn't use such a vehicle, nor did any of the other friendly militaries that were in the nation at the time, it was safe to assume that vehicle belonged to the enemy.

To solidify the fact that the Mi-8 was hostile, the front machine guns started flashing. Harvard stuck his fingers in his ears as fast as he possible could and fell flat on his chest as fast as he could. In almost the exact moment that he hit the tarmac, the anti-air battery unleashed a volley of missiles on the lone helicopter.

The ground shook, shockwaves from the barrage rattled the surrounding buildings, the vehicles, the men's very bones. Even with his fingers in his ears, nothing could spare anyone the ringing that followed the cannon fire from these weapons. It was a high pitched constant resonance of a bell that seemed to originate from inside the brain rather than the outside world. It was a sound every member of the armed forces became familiar with.

Harvard didn't get to watch the ordinance in flight, but he did manage to see the impact. Suddenly the helicopter flashed a brilliant white, followed by fiery reds and oranges as it split into many chunks of molten metal and shrapnel, plummeting to the ground in a symphony of violence.

Then the sound of the explosion hit. It was an unimpressive hard crack, nothing like the thunderous roar of the battery. Still, it was enough to startle half of the onlookers.

That was the first time Harvard had ever seen someone die. There was for him to know how many people were in that bird, nor was there a way for him to ever know who they were. They died nameless, and they shall be remembered as the nameless flight crew of the burning Mi-8.

CHAPTER 3 - GAMARRA

Breakfast came, as it always did, at 07:30 promptly. The DFAC was silent, seeming as if the entirety of Ulysses had nothing to say about the information that just recently came in. A rescue team was dispatched and reported that the Mi-8 had a crew of eight men, all who were killed from the initial explosion. Three of the killed were already wounded from a previous firefight. This helicopter was not a gunship like previously thought—it was an ambulance. More importantly, they weren't coming to attack Ulysses. They were running away.

Harvard stirred his cereal with a plastic spoon in complete silence. A block of lead had replaced his stomach, and yet still he felt like he could vomit. He had seen people die in movies and video games before, but never in person. The rational part of his mind nagged at him to move on given that they were still the enemy regardless of their passengers. He never even saw the corpses or the victims, just their swift, fiery destruction. Still, the fireball replayed itself in his mind with every blink.

All of the First Squad was seated at their usual spot without any conversation. Say for the silence, everything seemed normal.

Fern ate his exorbitantly large breakfast without a problem while Abram silently cooked his pork sausage MRE. Herbert and Carl took a bite of cereal or omelette every once in a while, but for the most part mirrored Harvard and just played with their food.

As Harvard's Wheat O's turned to a soggy lump of mush, Paul finally joined his men for breakfast. He didn't carry a tray of food with him, but instead a sloppily folded piece of paper. His gaze fell upon his trusted squad leader poking his mass of congealed wheat goop. Something about Harvard's glossed over stare into nothingness made the lieutenant's heart ache ever so slightly. "Well, hey guys." Paul forced his best facsimile of a smile as five pairs of eyes met his, "Uh… well, General Norton has decided that, due to recent events in the Southern Province, to start increasing our efforts into taking care of the Birkinistani threat."

Carl nudged Harvard gently with his elbow before whispering, "Who's General Norton?"

"Commander of the 152nd Infantry Division." He whispered back.

"Well, with the increase in the war effort, a lot of folks are getting real assignments today. We're no exception." Paul flicked a corner of the paper with his thumb to a steady cadence, his wine colored eyes surveying the emotionless faces of his men.

After a few moments of awkward silence, Harvard grunted as he set down his plastic spoon. He asked, "What do we have to do?" In a slightly agitated tone. Paul handed him the folded paper, which the squad leader didn't even bother reading. Without even hesitating, Harvard stuffed the paper into the chest pocket of his blouse.

Paul sighed, his gaze falling ever so slightly. "Well, direct orders from Norton himself. He wants you to pick up a letter from a contact named Klaus Lambert. He's supposed to be some high ranking official from the old Birkinistani government." Paul rubbed his forehead, displacing curls of blonde hair on his forehead.

"The democratic one or the fascist one?" Herbert asked quietly.

"The really weird one." Paul paused, "Anyways, he has a letter for General Norton regarding some important stuff. Sensitive information, enemy weapons caches, chemical processing plants, and, among other things, the location of General Saifullah."

The table instantly became quieter than silent. The men's eyes were fixed on Paul as if he were a Wise Man delivering the news of baby Jesus. Abram opened his mouth to speak, but closed it without saying a word.

Carl, who didn't seem too impressed, asked nonchalantly, "Who's General Saifullah?" Without hesitation, Harvard replied.

"Carl you're the one who brought up the Arlington Gas Attacks yesterday. Surely you know a thing or two about that." Harvard inquired. Carl tilted his head and furrowed his brow.

"Of course. Arlington, Texas. March 15th, 2004. 8,461 people died. I was nine years old when it happened." Carl explained. "Did he do that?" Harvard and Paul nodded.

"Yep. That bastardized shit sack organized the whole damn thing. He's the unholy lovechild of Hitler and Osama Bin Fucktard. Runs the entire nation, and there ain't jack shit the *real* government can do 'bout it." Abram snarled.

"And the worst part is that we have no idea where he is." Herbert added.

"Well… Until now, anyways." Paul smiled. Harvard furrowed his brow.

"That was perhaps the most cliche thing to say right there." Fern chimed in, mouth full of eggs.

"Screw you, man." The lieutenant chuckled.

"Wait," Harvard raised his hand to emphasize his point, "If such sensitive information is in that letter, why are you trusting a lowly infantry squad to pick it up?" His eyes fell upon Fern and Carl, "Specifically *our* infantry squad."

The lieutenant picked up Herbert's untouched bottle of orange juice, "It's not like you're going to be running into enemy fire to get it. It's a courier mission to Gamarra." He cracked the bottle's seal as he twisted it open, "Not like you're storming the beaches of Normandy… although maybe some of you would prefer that." He smiled at his platoon sergeant as he took a sip of juice, "Anyways, it should be fairly straightforward. Just don't lose the letter and you'll be fine. As always though, carry weapons just in case something bad does happen." Paul's eyes fell upon Harvard's lumpy mess of what used to be his breakfast. "Harv, you good?"

He quickly sputtered out, "Uh yeah. Just fine, sir." Even Harvard wasn't certain if that was a lie or not.

"If you insist." His voice was soft like a pastor's, "Well, you guys are signed out for 08:30. Finish up, gear up, et cetera. Good luck."

"Fifteen minute rule, so 08:15." Abram announced.

"Wait what?" Fern asked.

"Yeah, fifteen minute rule. If you're fifteen minutes early, you're on time, and if you're on time you're fifteen minutes late." Abram told him.

"But like, bro. Hold the on. That's like, not cool or fair." Abram slapped him on the back of the head, causing Harvard to recoil as flashbacks from the previous night's dinner played in his mind. He looked up and met his platoon commander's gaze, giving him a silent nod, signaling he understood his orders.

Harvard quietly stood up from his seat and asked, "Sir, am I free to go?" He wasn't certain why he was even asking. In the six months he had been stationed on Ulysses, he couldn't remember a single time he ever had to ask for permission to do anything. People just didn't care on this particular base, unlike every other military installation.

"Uh, sure. Go ahead." Paul returned with a tilted head and furrowed brow. Harvard respectfully nodded in response, then promptly exited the DFAC. The moment he crossed the border between the air conditioned dining hall and the outside world, an intense wave of heat smashed into him like a freight train. This wall of heat hit every soldier, every morning, and nobody ever got used to it.

Once he recovered from the sudden temperature differential, Harvard began wander aimlessly simply taking in the increase in activity. From every corner of the base, the presences of soldiers had seemingly doubled. Mechanics worked on their respective vehicles, readying them for missions that were probably far more interesting than simple courier duties. Platoons of infantrymen stood in formation in full kit—rifles, vests, helmets, everything they would possibly need for their tasks. It seemed that the helicopter had put everyone on high alert.

Eventually, he found his CHU. The desert sun had turned the metal door handle into the surface of the sun. In order to keep himself from burning his hands, Harvard kicked the door handle enough to twist it, then pushed the door open with his foot.

He quickly closed the door and flipped the switch to power the air conditioner. The CHU was only slightly cooler than the outside world, but the minuscule change in temperature was more then welcomed. A smile crept onto Harvard's face as cool air started flowing from the vents on the wall. He made his way to his bunk to start retrieving his gear from assorted bags and piles— among such items included his helmet, vest, backpack, and holster which all equated to roughly twenty-five pounds. This was only about half the gear he was expected to carry, which could range anywhere from forty to fifty pounds.

Then came the arduous task of actually putting everything on. No matter how many times he geared up for his almost daily patrols, he still had trouble with assembling his kit efficiently. Somewhere between struggling to buckle his vest and yelling at his helmet straps, the door opened letting out all the cold air, and letting in a Texan. "Hey Carl," He perked up like a puppy who had just heard his name, "You any good at putting on gear?" Harvard already knew what his response would be.

"Mhmm." And he was trapped. Harvard smirked and finished the arduous task of putting on half kit. He checked his pockets to make sure he had everything secure, tugged on his rigging, making sure nothing fell out, then turned around to find Carl struggling to put on his vest. He just stood there, watching the poor private figure out all the straps on his new vest. Everyone always said they know how to put on gear, everyone always struggled.

After a painstakingly long time, Carl managed to put everything on. He looked to Harvard and asked, "How much should I bring?" He had a bladed hand pointed towards his bunk which was almost overflowing with gear.

Harvard wanted to be mean and tell him to take everything, but instead opted to say, "Take only what you need. We're only going to be out for a few hours... probably." He shrugged, "Honestly I have no idea." Carl shrugged and left everything on top of his bed say for a little black leather journal and a nice looking pen. Harvard chuckled at his choice in comforts. He was a little bit disappointed that he didn't take everything, as that's what most new recruits do. Then one they're in the field, they realize how heavy everything is and find rather quickly they can't carry it all.

"Ready?" Harvard asked. The Texan simply nodded in response, and the two walked out of their residence and onto the surface of the sun. The world felt like it had been turned into an oven before, but now the men were sandwiched between two steel plates. Still, they pressed forward and made their way down to the HMMWV lot. There they would have to stand in the heat while they waited for the others.

"Harvard, I just noticed Ranger's missing." Carl and Harvard's eyes met, "Where'd he go?"

"Oh, right. Forgot to tell you. Sergeant Fernandez from Second Squad has him for an EOD refresher course right now. Captain Levi ordered the dogs for refreshers after the helicopter incident." Harvard smiled. He let his mind wander a bit, thinking about how little contact he actually had with Second and Third Squads. They were just enigmatic entities that floated around as statistics and nameless faces.

"Sounds like a good plan to me. IED sniffer who can't sniff IEDs would be bad." The private chuckled.

"Yeah that would kinda suck." Harvard wiped a bead of sweat from his forehead, "Like major suck."

Not too much longer the others arrived on foot, say for Paul who drove an HMMWV slowly behind them. The other enlisted members of the unit had equipment practically spilling out of their backpacks and vests, while Paul sat in the air conditioned HMMWV in standard ACUs. He wouldn't be accompanying them on this trip.

As Paul parked the vehicle a few meters from the men, Abram quickly inspected Harvard's kit for inconsistencies. It only took him a moment to spot a mistake, "Your vest isn't tight enough in the back, tip of your shoelace is sticking out of your right boot, and you have six magazines instead of nine." Harvard was about to open his mouth to protest, but the sergeant pierced him with his ice cold eyes. He then grunted and moved on to Carl.

"Do I even want to inspect you?" He asked.

"Yes, sergeant. I put a lot of effort into preparation." Carl smiled his typical politician's grin. Abram's eyes scanned the private's kit for inconsistencies, which he found plenty of.

"Holy fucking shit did you gear up in the latrine? I've seen *Fern* do a better job than you. Disgraceful." He grunted. The sergeant looked to Paul, who had stepped out of the HMMWV and was retrieving rifles from the trunk.

The lieutenant handed each of his men their rifle—M14 for Harvard, and M16s for the others. "Don't make me regret giving you this, glory hole pig." Abram growled with his eyes locked on Carl as Paul handed him his weapon. The private simply kept his grin until Abram broke eye contact with him to address their commander.

The men formed a line facing Paul with the HMMWV in the background in preparation for Paul's orders. He smiled, whether it was out of admiration or anxiety was a mystery. "Of all the men I've ever had under my command, you all have been the most fun to be around. I'm really proud to say I'm the commander of such a great unit." He cleared his throat, "That said, this is where I leave you for the afternoon. I know, I know, tragic." He paused in anticipation of laughter that never came. A disappointed sigh left his mouth, "You'll be taking this humvee behind me. Task should be pretty simple, go in, do the thing, get out. Shouldn't be dangerous at all, and if it is, something went *very* wrong. But I'm confident you can handle things if they go south." Harvard rolled his eyes. It had always been his belief that if First Squad ever got into a real combat situation, it would be Paul to get everyone killed. "Any questions on the mission?"

"Yeah I got one." Carl began to raise his hand.

"Shut the fuck up, Carl." Abram snarled. He pouted and returned his hand to his side.

The lieutenant began his conclusion to his mini speech, "If there are no questions, you are all dismissed. Good luck guys, and may God be with you." Harvard rolled his eyes once more. The men piled into the HMMWV with Harvard as driver, Abram in shotgun, and the other three squished into the back seat. As an almost unspoken decision, Carl was sandwiched between the two others, their rifles stack on top of each other like some amateur attempt at stacking firewood. The butt stock of a rifle was pressed against Carl's left cheek. He seemed to be taking things well enough, however, as he still had a smile on his face.

Suddenly, an idea popped into Harvard's head. "Sir!" He shouted, "I need the keys!" Paul quickly spun around, checking his pockets.

He looked back up to his soldier smiling, "Ah you bitch!" He laughed as the realization hit him. Abram chuckled a bit while the other three were too busy bickering over being smashed like sardines in a can. Harvard gave his commander a parting salute, then slowly drove off towards the front gate.

"I just want to point something out," Herbert spoke with his cheek smushed against his window, "We're nothing more than glorified mailmen." Harvard sighed, knowing full well that he was right. "Does that bother anyone else, or just me?" Harvard found himself nodding in agreement. Ulysses was a strange place—riflemen became mailmen, the enlisted should be officers, and the officers should be bagging groceries.

The vehicle came to a halt at the gate, and the two gate guards standing out front came to address the occupants. "Good morning, sergeant." One of the two, Private Delano, saluted Abram.

"Whoa! Dude, you don't salute NCOs, only lieutenant and higher." The second gate guard, Private Baker, quickly pushed his partner's hand back to his side.

"Right! Sorry!" Delano sighed, "When do you anticipate your return?"

Harvard glanced at Abram, "Uh…" Abram paused, "Probably 14:00. Probably."

"That's if we don't get blown up by an IED." Fern's voice was clear as day outside the HMMWV even though he was bread in a Carl sandwich.

"Man, fuck you Fern, I wasn't worried about that now I'm super fucking paranoid." Herbert punched him in the arm as best as he could with a Texan in his way.

"Seriously asshole, not cool." Harvard added.

"I wasn't worried about that until you brought that up. Now I'm worried." Carl said.

"Hey cum cunt, if Harvard drives over an IED, I'm gonna use you as a human meat." Abram growled.

"Well, I can see you all need serious psychological help... I mean, I can see you all need to get moving." Private Baker smiled.

"Nice save, bro." Private Delano high five'd his partner.

"Good luck, gentlemen! Hope you don't... explode." Private Baker's lips formed a grin similar to Carl's, prompting Harvard to roll up the window and drive off onto the open roads.

Thanks to Fern and Private Baker, Harvard found himself on high alert. His eyes constantly drifted to the sides of the road in search of anything suspicious. He had probably taken this highway hundreds of times during his first three months; never once did he have an incident before. Still, there was no shaking the paranoia, especially since the events of that morning.

The car was dead silent, say for the white noise of the wind rushing past the vehicle. The men were lost in thought, so transfixed on their minds and the images it conjured that the rest of the world didn't seem to matter. "Guys!" Fern shouted at the top of his lungs, causing the entire unit to jump at the sound.

"Jesus fucking Christ, Fern! What the fuck do you want?!" Harvard took a deep breath as his heart rate slowed.

"I've had a revelation!" Fern exclaimed, a huge grin on his face. Abram groaned.

"What the fuck could be so important that you make half the car shit their god damn pants?!" Abram sounded off. Harvard could physically feel his voice, which rubbed against his flesh like sandpaper.

"Get this. Black people… are like white people… but black." Perhaps what Harvard found the most infuriating about Fern's remark was how proud he looked in the rear view mirror. He sat upright with a triumphant smile on his face like he was Neil Armstrong after planting the flag on the moon.

"I don't like black people." Herbert yawned, "But at least they're not sand niggers."

"Racist!" Carl quickly snapped and pointed his finger at him.

"Shut the fuck up, Carl!" Herbert shouted.

"Really Herbert? You couldn't think of anything more creative to call them?" Harvard groaned, "Like firecracker? Raggedy Anne? Diaper Head? You had to resort to sand nigga."

"Well yeah, that's what they are."

"You're a fucking retard."

"You just learned that?" Abram chuckled.

"I mean no, I knew he was an asshole and racist but like, soft 'R' at least." Harvard sighed. "Hey Abram?"

"What?"

"If he says anything else racist, can you punch him in the dick?"

"If he says anything racist again, I'm gonna make you stop the car, I'm gonna throw him into the dirt, rip off his pants, and shove my boot so far up his asshole he'll be confused as to his sexuality and join the Navy!" Strings of spit flew from the sergeant's mouth, painting little streaks of wetness on the metal dashboard.

"You know what they say about the Navy." Fern smirked.

"You can take the sailor out of the Navy," Abram began, "But you'll never get the seaman out of him."

"Ew! No! I meant they have like, bro, they have like, good food 'n stuff!" Fern shouted. Abram began laughing a corse cackle that sounded like pain.

"Exactly!" He paused, "You get good food, then you go to the racks and it's a bunch of men with no women in sight. I mean, it's just what happens. You fork your food, then someone forks you."

"What did I sign up for?" Carl sighed.

"Not the Navy." Fern replied.

Harvard sighed quietly, "Dad was right. I should've been a doctor." He clenched the steering wheel tightly, "Stupid journalism major… stupid recruiter sticking me here." He grit his teeth, "I could've done better than this." The vehicle once again became silent with each of the men slowly drifting off into thought, except for Harvard. He focused all of his attention on the road, still paranoid from the thought of an IED. Dying was not too high on his priority list.

A bit of time passed in silence, probably only five minutes, but it felt like hours before anyone spoke again. A familiar southern drawl pierced the stillness, "Do we have any music?" Nobody replied for a moment. "I mean, we have a radio. Couldn't we play some music on like, an MP3 player or something?" Abram looked down at the center console radio and ran his gloved fingers across a few ports for assorted jacks and auxiliary cables.

"We do have an aux cord plugged in." He picked up a dusty black cable and waved the metal connector in the air. A smile formed on Harvard's face.

"Awesome. Pass it here." He took one hand off the wheel, palm facing upward.

"Dear fuck if you play 'Piano Man' again I'm going to shoot all five of us right now." Abram growled, "I'm playing some decent music."

"No you only play rock, and not the good kind either." Harvard slapped his hand back on the wheel, "I've never heard someone play so much ACDC in my life."

"What?! ACDC is the gospel of the fucking 11-Bravo! You're a disgrace to the brotherhood of the bayonet." The sergeant propped his legs up on the dashboard, "But, I'm 'aight with anything, just not Herbert's weird Jap shit." Without even needing to turn his his head, Herbert felt the burning sensation of Abram's glare.

"S-sorry." He whispered.

"Reggae?" Fern suggested, "Jah is love, Jah is life."

"And that. I will not have that hippie shit playing in *my* war zone."

"I've downloaded a few Queen songs. 'Bohemian Rhapsody', 'Don't Stop Me Now', 'Under Pressure', the like. Anyone up for that?" Carl waived his small MP3 player in the air so that Harvard could see in the rear view mirror.

"Carl, are you secretly in the Navy?" Herbert asked.

"What?"

"He's calling you gay, faggot." Abram grunted. The private shrugged.

Harvard sighed, "So we really have no idea what to play because everyone hates each other's music."

"Sounds about right." Abram shifted his boots uncomfortably on the dashboard.

"Typical." Herbert grunted.

Fern inhaled deeply, ready to spout some nonsense, "Music is a way of life. We should embrace all sorts of ideas and… like, play some music. Someone pass the aux cord."

"No!" Abram, Harvard, and Herbert all shouted in unison while Carl sat silently, staring out the window.

He stayed transfixed on the outside world; nothing but desert and wasteland existed past the thin metal walls of the HMMWV. "Do you guys miss home?" He asked in that hauntingly innocent tone. Nobody answered him, so he simply continued speaking. "I mean, day in, day out, this is your lives." He paused, "Our lives. Huh. Guess I forget where I am sometimes."

"How can you forget?" Herbert asked. A faint smile formed on the new private's face.

"It's easy. I just like thinking 'bout what's back in the States. The good parts, anyways." He traced the seams of the vinyl seats with his fingers, eyes still gazing into the sandy badlands with the wonderment of a child. "Lot's of good back home. That's what I like focusing on. Lot's to love, lot's to miss."

The men relapsed into silent contemplation, each pondering a different question of the universe. "I don't miss it." Abram's voice was as cold as ice. "What's there to miss? Back home our kind ain't liked. We're just baby killers to 'em." He leaned up against his door, "I don't really blame 'em. Civies don't understand what we do. They see the before and after, but not the during." He started laughing as he too began gazing out the window. "Man I joined the army almost nineteen years ago! I've been doing this shit for as long as you and Fern have been alive!" Still, nobody replied. Perhaps it was out of respect, perhaps it was out of apathy, nobody dared break the sergeant's monologue. "I remember it like it was yesterday too. My dad was so damn proud of me. He was an NCO back in the first Gulf War, my grand-pappy was a fuckin' Command Sergeant Major back in 'Nam. You should'a seen 'im. Fuckin' badass—my hero growing up." He let out a long winded sigh, "But he told me stories of when he got back in '71. People spat at him, accused him of all sorts of thangs. 'Baby killer. Baby killer! *Baby killer!*" His voice exploded in the tiny vehicle, but was soon followed by an equally deafening silence to the point that it even drowned out the ambient sounds of the road. Just as it seemed impossible to break this silence, Abram shattered it, "So I don't miss America one bit. I'd die for her, sure, and I'd do so without hesitation. But I don't miss her. She sure as hell don't miss us."

CHAPTER 4 - FIVE MEN IN A VALLEY

The HMMWV's breaks squealed as the vehicle slowed to a halt in the parking lot of the Gamarra HQ. Outside the windows of the car civilians in traditional garbs walked the streets, going about their daily routines. American military policemen dotted the street corners in their green digital patterned uniforms, acting as the only police force the town had seen in decades. The city was beautiful —a stunning example of what happens when civilians and the military can accomplish together. Gamarra truly was paradise.

"This place is a fucking dump." Abram growled as he unbuckled his seatbelt. "Everyone out, we have shit to do. We're securing the perimeter of the town to make sure…" he raised his fingers in the air to create air quotes, "'the area is secure for the VIP.' Fucking disgusting." He glared at Harvard, who sat stationary in the driver's seat, "Understood?"

"Y-yes, sergeant!" Harvard killed the engine and practically flew out of the vehicle. The others followed suit to form a line arm's length apart in front of the HMMWV. The revered platoon sergeant stood directly in front of them, centered neatly between the four junior enlisted men.

He glared at his men with a burning fire in his eyes—a fire the boys could physically feel scorching their very souls. "Okay fucktards, listen closely because I'm only doing this once. We're meeting our contact at 11:00 hours which gives us about three hours to walk around the perimeter as per our security orders." He focused his laser vision on Fern, "This is mainly for PT. I'd say you've fallen out of shape, but that implies you were once in shape." A few moments of awkward silence passed as the junior enlisted men slowly turned to face Fern. "Fern I'm calling you a fucking fat ass."

"Thank you."

"Fuck you!" He shifted his focus to the squad as a whole once more, "Fall in, staggered column. Guns down until I say so, *Carl*." Without hesitation, the men formed a trapezoid behind Abram with Harvard standing off to his five O'clock and Carl taking last man.

Then they started marching. Not a word was said as they moved through the city; they simply let their minds wander from thought to thought. It's not like they had anything better to do, they were in the safety of the town, so they didn't need to stay on high alert. Eventually, however, they did reach the main gates of the town. They had crossed the border that separated the town from the desolate wasteland that was Birkinistan.

Harvard had hardly noticed the heat until then. In the short five minutes it took to walk from the HMMWV to the desert, he had sweat so much it looked like he had jumped into a pool. It wasn't just him either, it was all of the men. Each of them had perspired enough liquid to fill a canteen. It didn't help in the slightest that the weight of their gear forced the men to exert more precious energy. Still, as painful as the heat was, it couldn't drown out the sound of boots on coarse dirt—an omnipresent reminder of the desert.

In an effort to distract himself from the heat, Harvard turned his head to face Abram and asked, "Hey sarge, you alright?" He didn't reply, so the private pressed further, "I only ask because of the stuff you said in the car. Seemed a bit out of character for you." All Abram did was wipe some sweat from the back of his perfectly bald head. "I don't think I've ever heard you talk about… y'know… feelings and shit."

Abram let out a long, deep winded sigh. "I'm fine, Harvard." He grumbled, "I'm just getting old."

"You're 36."

"Fuck off." He didn't say this in his normal berating tone, but rather a somber and weary one, "I've just been doing this for a while. 19 years, 12 tours of duty in four different countries. I've had a good run." His eyes fell upon the dusty horizon.

"Something tells me you're not satisfied with that." Harvard's voice was softer than silk.

"We should be content with serving our country." He shifted his gaze to the squad leader as best as he could without turning his body, "I'm just getting older, but I don't want to leave until the war is over. They're either taking me home with a victory or in a body bag."

"We'll get that victory. Good guys win, right?" Carl chirped.

"Ah, my dear Carl. Good and evil are simply concepts made up by people to dictate social action. In the grand scheme of the universe, there are only events." Herbert's voice scraped the inside of Harvard's skull. He clenched his rifle tightly, hating himself for agreeing with him.

"Not necessarily." Fern's overly laid back voice accentuated his pseudo-philosophical tone, "If we think about the Many Worlds Interpretation, then the concepts of good and evil may very well be ingrained in the fabric of space-time. If everything with a non-zero probability happens, then it is entirely possible that, given enough trials, a universe becomes self aware and creates it's own system of right and wrong based upon it's own ideals." Harvard turned his head to see that those words really did come out of Private Fern's mouth.

"I want to remind everyone that this is the same dude who thought a peanut butter and tuna sandwich was a good idea." He smirked as he refocused his attention to the world in front of him.

Herbert let a snobbish laugh escape his lips, "But are we to assume that the Many Worlds Interpretation is correct? Have you not heard of the famous Schrödinger's Cat thought experiment?" He paused for dramatic effect, "It is entirely possible that only this one universe exists, and that every time the superposition of a wave function is broken, every possible outcome of the wave function collapses into the *true* outcome." Harvard grit his teeth as Herbert butchered quantum mechanics, "So, if this is the only universe that exists, then the concept of right and wrong are—"

"If you two don't shut the fuck up right now, I'm gonna stick my foot up both your asses and wear you around like a couple of autistic flip flops!" At the sergeant's order, everyone returned to silence.

Almost as an act of defiance, the world became excruciatingly loud. A single crack echoed over the mountainside. A single, unmistakeable crack. Harvard's heart jumped into his throat, his mind started running faster than the speed of sound. Someone just shot.

The first bang was followed by another, and then another, and then another until the entire hillside lit up with the sound of machine guns. The entire patrol halted and crouched down as the shooting increased, each man focusing their attention to the source of the gunfire.

It was surreal the way everything happened. Harvard had heard shooting before while he was in Gamarra, or on base, or on a patrol when he was miles upon miles away but this? This was the closest he had ever been to a real firefight. His mind refused to accept that the engagement was just beyond the top of the hill he stood on—probably not even more than a kilometer away. Within a thousand meters, real people, with real guns, were locked in a fight for their lives—kill or be killed.

He so desperately wanted to help his fellow soldiers, but he found his boots glued to the dirt, their rubber soles melted in place by the desert sun. He could only stand there, with his weapon in hand, listening to his brothers in green fight for their lives. The sounds of the conflict increased in intensity, punctuated by thumps of explosives. The desire to push onward ate away at the melted rubber and petrified muscles until he finally managed to take a step forward.

Instantly Harvard felt bile rise in his throat, but he pushed it down as he took another labored step closer to the crest in the hill. War drowned the endearing sound of crackling gravel beneath boots as the entire squad managed to push forward, even if it was at a snail's pace.

He kept his head on a swivel, partially to search for hostiles, but mainly to keep an eye on his companions. Each of them fiddled with their weapons, licked their lips, bit their cheeks, or squinted, say for Abram who was laser focused what was in front of him.

Then the world called the command "halt" with the guttural sound off of a deafening explosion. The ground shook, smacking Harvard hard in the chest. His ears rang with tinnitus, whistling the tune of war. As the bells in his head slowly faded out of existence, the desert fell into a crypt like silence. Even with the ball of fire beating upon them, the entire squad felt an ice cold shiver chill them to their souls.

A single footstep bursted Harvard's eardrums. He quickly turned his head to find Abram slowly creeping forward, taking great caution as to not disturb the mournful tranquility any more than he already had. The rest of the squad followed suit, treading lightly as if the entire hillside was covered in landmines.

Harvard swallowed, flicking the safety of his rifle on and off. He knew that Abram wouldn't have stepped forward if they weren't going to investigate the conflict and perhaps recover some wounded soldiers or enemy materiel. They wouldn't know until they got there.

A crack echoed over the mountainside, stopping the men in their tracks. A familiar sense of dread washed over Harvard like rainfall. Then came another, and half a second later came another.

There was no mistaking what just happened. They knew there wouldn't be any more shots echoing over the mountains, no wounded soldiers to recover, no materiel left to gather. They knew they had failed their fellow man. A voice lost to memory asked, "Should we pursue them?"

"No." Abram replied, his voice more corse than the dirt beneath their boots. "It's not worth it." He began walking forward without the rest of the squad. The junior enlisted men all addressed each other silently as if to ask each other how they were doing with a simple glance. Each of them shifted uncomfortably, or fidgeted with their weapons, or glanced down at their boots every couple of seconds. Without saying a word, the men simultaneously started walking to catch up with their sergeant.

Just before they reached the crest of the hilltop, Abram stuck his left arm our bent at a 90 degree angle with a closed fist. The men halted. He addressed Fern with a bladed hand, directing him to the break in the hill. The private silently complied with the order without question or hesitation, and carefully crept to his position. Ten agonizing seconds later, he reported in. "Clear!" He shouted. At once, the entire squad stopped holding their breaths. They each moved up to the crest to assess the situation.

Beneath the squad was a narrow valley with incredibly steep hills on either side, just wide enough for a dirt road to pass through. Vegetation grew on the ridges which could easily obscure an ambush, which was precisely what happened. Only about three hundred yards away, the mangled remains of an HMMWV was smashed into a boulder off the side of the road. The entire chassis was disfigured by a launcher weapon, evident by the shrapnel that was strewn about the desert like a child's sandbox. The blood soaked corpse of an American soldier laid halfway out of the HMMWV's shattered windshield on the passenger's side, intestines lazily flopped onto the remnants of the hood. The soldier resembled a fish after it had been caught and cleaned on the deck of a boat.

Next to the wreckage and facing the ridge where Harvard and the others sat, the bodies of three other soldiers laid face down in the dirt. Their uniforms had been torn to pieces and scattered amongst the shrapnel from the wreckage, leaving them completely naked. Most of their gear was taken, and what wasn't was haphazardly thrown around or half buried in the sand. Even from the distance, Harvard could tell that the back of the soldier's heads were missing. They had been executed.

A gust of wind wafted the most putrid stench Harvard had ever smelled into his nostrils. It was horrible, like a wet dog was mixed with a cheap perfume and rotting meat. It was so terrible it made his eyes water.

He knelt down to rest his mind, bracing himself with his left hand on the dirt, only he didn't meet the hard ground as expected. It was squishier and moist. Harvard checked his hand and fell backwards, adrenaline coursing through his veins. Instantly he shrieked and fell backwards, kicking himself away from his previous position.

"Harvard what's wr—oh my God that's disgusting." Fern averted his eyes from Harvard as fast as he could, shielding his face with his left hand. Herbert gagged while Carl helped Harvard to his feet. Abram picked up the source of the disgust, and once it registered in his head he dropped it with a yelp.

"That's a fucking human leg!" Abram kicked it as hard as he could, sending it spinning off into the valley like a soccer ball. The men searched the immediate area and found the dismembered corpse of a Birkinistani soldier, limbs ripped off from an M203 40 millimeter high explosive grenade. He was almost unrecognizable with most of his face and torso seemingly vaporized by the blast.

That was when, for the second time in two days, Harvard threw up. His rifle thumped against the ground while he wretched and heaved a foul yellow ooze from his mouth. Carl stood by him, making sure his friend was alright, while the others secured the surrounding perimeter. Eventually the private finished his heaving, retrieved his weapon, and got back in formation.

Another breeze of desert wind kicked up some sand in the valley, covering the corpses in a thin layer of tan dust. The sand crept into every crevice of the HMMWV, the holes in the deceased men's heads, their misplaced gear, everything. The desert even found it's way into the living's gear as well, clogging the seams where their canteen lids screwed on, peppering the tiny brims on their glasses, invading the cracks where their boots were bloused over their trousers.

The squad's battle hardened sergeant spat out a loogie full of saliva and dirt. He didn't seem to be phased much after the initial freak out with the severed leg. He kept his eyes peeled, checking flanks, the rear, the front, all while flicking the select fire of his rifle from safe to fire over and over again as though he were clicking a push-pen. He tapped his toe box on the dirt in quick and consecutive intervals to the beat of the drums in his mind.

The other junior enlisted seemed in a daze, say for Carl. He was peculiar, staring directly at the American corpses, hardly even blinking. His right hand clenched the pistol grip of his rifle, his left gently resting on the bottom of the hand guard, thumb running up and down along the smooth polymer. His brow was furrowed, breaths short yet unpronounced, almost like he was under a spell.

"Carl?" Harvard whispered. He cocked his head ever so slightly, just enough to be able to make eye contact with his friend. "You okay?"

"Yeah." He did nothing to hush his tone, "Just weird to think this is real."

The dead stillness of the desert returned. The tan rocks of the wasteland were the tombstones of the deceased men who laid in the valley. Their eulogy would be the silence. Their undertaker would be the wind. Five lives were ended in that valley. Five sons. Five brothers.

CHAPTER 5 - KLAUS

The men returned to the safety of the town drenched from head to toe in a thick layer of sweat and grease, each of them still dazed from the events in the valley. The late morning sun scorched the world, just barely sitting beneath the threshold in which sand turns to glass. The white concrete buildings in Gamarra did little, if anything, to offer protection from the heat. In fact, the whitewashed walls reflected the light off of them, propagating the heat further.

A familiar lead block replaced Harvard's stomach. The sour taste of bile sat upon his tongue, his body ached from over encumbrance. He didn't even feel in control of his actions anymore; he simply stared through the eyes of a man named Reginald Harvard. Even this didn't fully describe the nature of this out-of-body sensation. It was more like he was watching himself in third person—an invisible follower observing a body he once called his own.

The squad trudged through the town, staggering through mobs of people like jungle vines in Vietnam, avoiding fellow soldiers like landmines dug in deep. Eventually they found the town square—a roughly 100 by 100 yard square with the most quaint little mosque in the center. The ground underfoot was once tiled with gorgeous polished sandstone, but time and war has since weathered away what beauty remained. Now it was only a scuffed and abused testament to the years of conflict the country had faced.

The crackling of Abram's radio brought everyone back to reality, "All callsigns, this is Crossroads, be advised. Birkinistani forces have been spotted in the foothills between Gamarra and Al Hashu, over." The voice on the other end sounded to be a Swedish man with a heavy, but understandable, accent.

Abram grabbed ahold of his radio and pressed the transmit button, "Crossroads, this is Alpha-One-One, we found the corpses of four Americans and one mangled Haji at 160141 marching around out there on patrol. Send 'em back to their families, over."

"Copy Alpha-One-One, we'll dispatch cleanup. Anything else we can do for you, over?" Harvard sighed as he waited for his platoon sergeant to stop playing with the radio.

"Negative, Crossroads. Alpha-One-One out." There was a single beep from the radio signaling Crossroads understood his last message and he was dismissed.

"Humph." Herbert grunted, "So *now* they tell us the goat gropers are out there."

"Bro, like, just be glad they didn't shoot us." Fern's very existence made Harvard want to sock him in the jaw.

"Can it, chucklefuck. We have shit to do." Abram began walking forward into the town square with the rest of the squad following closely behind.

The sergeant guided his men to an older gentleman sitting on a wooden park bench that was secured to the ground with a few black iron rivets. He wore a light green polo tucked into his jeans with a brown belt. His jet black hair was parted to the side, although his head was titled at such an angle that it obscured his face from view. Upon closer inspection, Harvard determined that this man had fallen asleep in the desert sun, although it was just as likely he passed out from heat exhaustion.

Abram cleared his throat, jostling the man awake. "Good morning, sir. You are Klaus Lambert, Chief of Foreign Council for the Emir of Birkinistan. Is this correct?"

The man yawned audibly, "Ya ya. Zat's me." Harvard stopped paying attention to the conversation and instead focused on his boots. The dust of the desert couldn't cover the noticeable blood stain on his left toe box. It was only a drop—no larger than a pencil's width—but the dark crimson splatter leapt off the tan canvas of the boot.

"We're from Ulysses Airfield, US Army. We have direct orders from General Norton to retrieve a letter you have for him. Is this correct?" Abram's voice sounded like razor blades on a chalk board.

Klaus smiled and reached into his back pocket, "You're early." He still did not produce the letter.

"Heh. That's what she said." Fern giggled.

"Come on man, that's not funny." Carl said.

"It was a little."

"Lock it down, twat buckets!" The platoon sergeant snapped at his men. He sighed and refocussed his attention on Klaus.

Harvard looked up from his boots to finally make eye contact with their target, but he never made it past his mustache. There was something horribly wrong with his facial hair. He had a toothbrush mustache to accompany his jet black side parting hair. "Oh no." Harvard whispered and snapped his gaze to Herbert.

To say he was awestruck would be an understatement. The specialist stared with his jaw wide open, eyes sparkling brighter than fireworks. "Mein..." he muttered and stuttered pathetically as he attempted to form sentences out of the thoughts in his mind.

"For the love of Christ please shoot me." Harvard whispered, "Sergeant, can we please just get the letter and get going?" Abram only grunted in response.

"Mister Lambert, if you could please hand over the letter, we can be on our way." Harvard managed to say. Klaus sighed and finally produced the sealed white envelope that contained the prize the men sought.

As Abram and Harvard turned to walk away, Klaus let out a long winded sigh. "Kids zees days. Von't even humor an old man for his shtory."

"I will, sir!" Even though he wasn't looking at him, Harvard knew Herbert had the biggest, stupidest grin on his face. "Please, tell me your secrets, my dear sir."

"For the love of Christ please shoot him." Harvard whispered just loud enough for his sergeant to hear.

"Herbert, I just wanted to let you know that every night I stand over your bed with a pillow thinking about how easy it would be to smother you in your sleep. So for the love of *fuck* get your ass in gear or I will beat you to death with your own skull." An icy chill ran up Harvard's spine as the words left Abram's mouth. There was something inherently frightening when the sergeant was calm with his threats rather than screaming.

"But sarge!" He turned to face Abram. "What if he gives us valuable information on how to kill the enemy? Oh! What if he tells us the secret to cleansing the Jews?!" As the words left his mouth, the butt stock of Harvard's rifle slammed into his head with enough force to knock him to the ground. His helmet thumped against the sandstone, gear clanking and rattling as his body came to a rest. The spectacle instantly attracted stares from all the civilians occupying the square.

Harvard turned to address the squad. "Um... he tripped on his boot laces."

"Right." Abram agreed.

"I didn't see anything." Fern turned his head to face some women off in the distance of the square.

"What happened? I wasn't paying attention." Carl put a black leather notebook back into his backpack pocket. Evidently Carl really wasn't paying attention, which was probably for the best considering he would likely be the one to tattle on him for bashing a fellow soldier.

Harvard returned his attention to Klaus, "Look, we're not in a good mood today so I'll make this quick. Shave your fucking mustache. You look like Adolf Hitler." With that as their closing remarks, Harvard and Abram picked up the collapsed Herbert and dragged his limp body from the square to the HMMWV.

~ ~ ~

The trip back was as uneventful as the trip away. For the longest time the vehicle sat in a deep silence, everyone lost in their thoughts, pondering mysteries and philosophies without words ever leaving their lips. Harvard couldn't speak for the others, but he still felt the drumming in his chest as his mind fixated on the events in the valley and on the mountainside.

In his almost meditation-like state, he asked himself a single question: "Could I have done something?" He repeated this over and over again in his mind. He had no idea if there was anything he realistically could do, and even if he tried if it would change anything. If he perhaps decided to play hero, he very well could've gotten himself killed, or even worse, his friends.

But as he further thought about the events, a new question manifested itself: "Could I have pulled the trigger?". He needed not to repeat this like the last. It was something he never truly questioned before. He liked to pretend he could pull the trigger to end another man's life either to protect himself or someone he cared about, but he never had the opportunity to test that. It wasn't a matter of if he could land the shot in the first place, as he could hit a quarter at nearly five-hundred yards, and a human sized target at a thousand. It was all the psychological side of killing.

Still, Harvard wasn't a killer. The mere thought of taking someone's life was nauseating. But that was the job he signed up for, so if the need came when he had to shoot someone, he knew he would have to. Living with himself afterwards would be a completely different story.

In some strange way, he felt like he contributed to the deaths of those four men in the valley. By his logic, he allowed himself to become frozen, bones to lead and muscles to concrete. He repeated the question from before: "Could I have done something?" Whether or not his actions were correct was something he would have to live with.

In the briefest of moments between thoughts, a cardboard box sitting on the road snapped Harvard back to reality. Without a word of warning to his passengers, he swerved the HMMWV out of the path of the box to avoid driving over it. The men screamed, being broken from their silent pondering so violently and forcefully thrown against the doors of the vehicle. Helmets smacked into each other producing audible, and in any other situation comical, thumps and thuds. Harvard slammed the gas pedal as hard as he could, lurching the vehicle forward in an attempt to get away from the box as fast as possible.

But that's all it was: a simple cardboard box. No explosive shockwave followed, no cloud of smoke floated upward behind the car, just a small tan cardboard box sitting in the road. No IEDs, no traps, nothing—just an HMMWV full of terrified soldiers and an empty desert that toyed with them. "Sorry... sorry." Harvard bit his bottom lip, "I thought it was a bomb." He dared not meet the gaze of his passengers in the rear view mirror.

With a deep breath, Harvard returned to the land of thought, drifting from idea to idea without repercussions. But he found his mind drift to the potential dangers that were all around him. The mountains on either side were less than a kilometer away, and could have patrols of Birkinistani soldiers sat waiting for the perfect opportunity to ambush an unescorted and unarmed HMMWV, just like the one he and his friends sat in.

Then his thoughts turned to the Mi-8 that flew over Ulysses. Before that morning, intelligence suggested that Birkinistan only had a few MiGs from the cold war, but seeing helicopters meant that the enemy was stronger than they were initially thought to be. At any moment another Mi-8, even a Hind, could spot the HMMWV and blows it to bits and pieces without a second thought.

A drop of sweat fell from Harvard's brow and splashed upon the steering wheel. Harvard wasn't sure if it was the heat or his own mind making him anxious, but he wasn't happy about it. The worrisome thought was that any number of unforeseen events— from ambushes to mechanical failures—could unexpectedly occur, leaving his friends and him in the middle of the wasteland without any hope of a rescue for hours.

Soon enough, the top of Ulysses' air traffic control tower poked it's head out form behind the foothills surrounding the HMMWV. Harvard breathed a sigh of relief. The spire made him feel a little safer, as he figured nobody would be stupid enough to ambush a single unarmed vehicle so close to an active military installation. For as far as he was concerned, he was protected from the worst the Birkinistanis could throw at him.

~ ~ ~

The vehicle came to a stop in the parking lot. The engine died, prompting everyone to start slowly piling out. "God damn…" Herbert groaned as he slowly climbed out of the car, "Why does my head hurt like shit?"

"You tripped on your boot laces when you were talking to Mister Lambert." Carl smiled, his face had a streak mark of dried dirt crossing his left cheek.

"Seriously?" Herbert ran his hand through his hair, cradling his rifle and helmet in the other. "Must've been some fall."

"It was. Pretty funny honestly." Harvard chuckled. He turned to face Abram, "So are we going to debrief Paul together, or just you, just me, how do we want to do this?"

The platoon sergeant removed his helmet to rub his shiny bald head, "You and me go." He addressed Fern, "Hey shit head, take our guns back to the armory." He tossed his rifle at the private who stumbled around to catch it. Harvard, in comparison, politely handed him his.

"Thanks Fern." Harvard began walking away with Abram, looking back only to wave to the others. He forgot what he was supposed to do with his hands as he walked, given that his rifle was no longer with him. Beyond the fences of Ulysses, his rifle was the only thing separating him from an enemy's bullet. On base, however, carrying a weapon wasn't allowed. There was a strange, humorous aspect of life in Birkinistan—the war zone could go from excruciatingly stressful to excruciatingly boring in a matter of moments.

The ball of fire in the sky radiated down upon the world, as it always did, and as it always will. The short walk from the parking lot to the Lower Offices was enough to completely exhaust much of Harvard and Abram's energy. Not that their stamina was a concern of anyone on base; the airfield was busier than it ever was before with soldiers carrying out their orders and actually getting things done.

Eventually the two found the entrance to the Lower Offices, prompting Harvard to hold the door open for his superior. The moment his hand touched the metal handle, he felt like his nylon gloves hand melted away, fusing both his hand to the glove and the door handle. All of that subsided the moment he stepped foot into the building as the air conditioning wafted over him, pocking his skin with goosebumps. Both soldiers couldn't help but let a smile creep on their faces.

Abram and Harvard made their way to Paul's cubicle, but found that it was empty, and a complete disaster. Papers were strewn everywhere, his computer was left logged in and on a spreadsheet marked "Classified Spreadsheet 31-6", and a few books either sitting on the floor or were still open to a particular page. If Paul had left a note detailing where he would be, it would be near impossible to find in all the clutter. "There is no way I'm cleaning this up." Harvard whispered to himself.

Abram tapped a lieutenant on the shoulder, "Excuse me, ma'am, do you know where First Lieutenant Paul is?"

She furrowed her brow before replying, "Last I heard he was seeing General Norton. Something about a letter with General Saifullah's location and stuff."

"Yeah we just got back from picking that up." Harvard chimed in.

"Awesome! Great work, 'gents" She chuckled.

"Thank you, ma'am. Means a lot comin' from you." Neither Abram or Harvard knew anything about this lieutenant.

"Of course. Hope you find your LT." She smiled and walked off without another word.

Abram bumped Harvard with his elbow, "That right there is a good lieutenant."

"How so?" Harvard replied, just idly watching the other soldiers in the office.

"First of all, she was polite and respectful to us. She obviously knows that the army couldn't run without the enlisted men, so she doesn't treat us like shit. And did you see that smile? An actual, genuine smile for a job well done. She treats us like human beings, but I can tell she knows how to fill her roll as a lieutenant too. All in all, good lieutenant." Abram noticed that Harvard was looking at one particular soldier. He traced his gaze and found that he was looking at a female red haired soldier with pale skin who was talking to one of the M3 commanders.

Harvard recognized her from the hanger that morning. The man she was talking to was probably her commander. Perhaps she too just got back from a mission and was debriefing him. He noticed she finished talking to the officer, and turned around, eyes immediately meeting Harvard's. He quickly looked at his boots, but peaked back up and found that she was still looking at him. He smiled, she smiled back, and suddenly Harvard felt butterflies in his stomach. Then he felt a hand hit him on the back with an audible thud, alerting a few nearby officers.

"Harvard, do you find that soldier attractive?" Abram asked quietly.

"Y-yes sergeant." Harvard found himself stuttering, his face turning completely red. He looked up at his sergeant awaiting a response.

"So you're crushing on a cav scout, huh? Fucking despicable. And she's a ginger? Come on, Harvard, that's just gross."

"She just reminds me of someone I knew, okay?"

"Heh. Fuckin' pussy." They resumed their walk out of the building and out onto the blistering airfield.

At last they found themselves at the entrance and quickly opened the doors to spare their hands. Goosebumps once again pocked the men's skin as the temperature dropped to something comfortable. They walked almost angrily through the lobby and to the steel door. Abram acknowledged each officer with a "Good afternoon sir/ma'am" with respect to gender, while Harvard ignored everything. He let his mind wander for just a moment, and it brought him back to the mutilated corpse of the Birkinistani soldier.

To say Harvard was angry was an understatement. He didn't even knock on General Norton's door, just walked right in with Abram staring wide eyed at his soldier—blown away that he had the nerve to disrespect a general like that. Harvard figured that if the old man didn't want anyone walking in, he would've closed the door.

"Anyways, that's the plan. Any questions, Lieutenant?" General Norton finished. Harvard didn't care.

"No sir. It's very solid and well thought out. My men are ready to assist in any way we can." Harvard felt his stomach churn with his lieutenant's volunteering. He cleared his throat, prompting both the officers to address the enlisted men standing in the back of the office.

"Oh, uh… Hi Harvard. Hi Abram. Welcome back." Paul sat staring with a dumb look on his face, "We missed you."

Abram groaned, "Come on man, don't make it weird."

"Gentlemen," Norton paused for dramatic effect, "I trust you secured the letter from Klaus?" Harvard gazed into the two, piercing blue eyes in the General's skull. His skin was covered in wrinkles from age and stress, hair grayed in a professional and well kept style. Behind those eyes held decades of war that defined this man, and anyone with half a sense of empathy could see it.

"Yes sir." Abram reported, passing the envelope to Paul who sat it down on the desk. General Norton looked up at the two soldiers with a faint grin on his face.

"Good! Good." The old general's voice was cold and corse from years of duty. Abram grunted, reminding Harvard who really had the gruffest of voices.

Paul attempted one of Carl's signature smiles, "Well, I say job well done. Since you're here, wanna do the debrief now? General Norton and I may be a while."

"Let's just do it now. Get it done." Harvard replied, bitterness in his voice. The lieutenant raised an eyebrow at his private.

"Alright, well, let's start with the basics. Obviously the mission was successful, you got the letter, and I assume that all of you came back right? Any shots fired?" Paul asked.

"All men accounted for, no casualties, no combat. Humvee is in perfect condition, all weapons have been returned to the arms room. Mission objective secured. All contacts were cooperative. Specialist Gerolf Herbert suffered a minor injury when he tripped over his untied shoelaces and knocked himself unconscious for several minutes after his head struck the ground." Harvard reported, suppressing a smirk as he replayed whacking Herbert in the head in his mind.

"Excellent! I'm happy to hear the mission went well!" Paul smiled. He turned to face the general and added, "See, I told you my men were great."

General Norton was still cold, but with a smile replied, "I never once doubted them. Private, do you have anything else to report?"

Harvard sighed, knowing that he had to report the conflict in the valley. "Yes, sir. While carrying out a perimeter walk around Gamarra we heard a firefight relatively close. We investigated the scene after the firing ceased to discover a neutralized humvee, four KIA Americans, and one KIA Birkinistani. We were unable to recover the bodies." His knees began to feel weak under his own weight. The atmosphere in the office thickened, light seeming to drain out the windows instead of pour in.

The two officers studied each other's face for a time. Harvard simply stood there waiting for someone to say something to reassure him. He would only get General Norton's murmur, "Well… shit."

"Sir, we radio'd Crossroads and he said he's dispatched a clean up crew." Abram reported.

Silence washed over the office once more as the men simply stared at each other. Eventually Abram asked, "Are we dismissed, gentlemen?" General Norton simply nodded in response. The enlisted men snapped to attention and saluted their superiors, prompting Paul to stand and salute as well. General Norton simply saluted while sitting in his chair. With that as their parting remarks, Abram and Harvard swiftly exited General Norton's office.

CHAPTER 6 - THE BOY IN THE BLACK SHIRT

Four days had gone by with First Squad doing nothing productive like usual. At least not from a war standpoint, Harvard finished his last unread book and Carl managed to make Abram laugh at a joke —as punishment he was forced to do fifty pushups. Other than that, however, there was nothing notable that happened.

The rest of Birkinistan was not nearly as stagnant. The activity on Ulysses increased exponentially; other infantry teams were sent on twice as many patrols that were four times as long, convoys of HMMWV's escorted by armor platoons came and went almost hourly, and the sound of helicopters and fixed winged aircraft became so frequent that it wasn't even annoying anymore.

The enemy too increased their efforts. Firefights became more frequent, echoing off the mountains surrounding the base. The hospital had a steady stream of injured men checking in and checking out with anything from gunshot wounds to severed limbs. The thing that unsettled everyone the most was nightly display of two or three wooden boxes with flags draped over them, sobbing friends kneeling by their sides.

It was 21:49, the sun had long since disappeared, but the airfield was still as busy as New York City during lunch rush hour traffic. That wasn't Harvard's problem, as he was absolutely exhausted from a long day of pretending to be doing something important. In actuality, he spent the entire day throwing rocks at empty soda cans with Paul. Just ten minutes prior, all the infantry officers were called to a mandatory meeting, so Paul had to depart.

With nothing better to do, he returned to his CHU to find Carl had somehow brought Ranger up to the top bunk with him. They were sound asleep, Carl cuddling Ranger like a plush toy. A small smile formed on Harvard's face at the sight. "Sleep tight, you two." He whispered. He knew the Texan would need all the rest he could get—he had a long thirteen months ahead of him.

Harvard's attention was caught by a small black journal sitting on top of Carl's duffle bag. It was still open to a page marked with the day's date, covered in scribbles and near illegible handwriting. He wasn't aware that Carl was keeping a journal. Something told him to read it, but at the same time he knew he shouldn't. Still, the temptation lingered, festered and slowly ate away at him until he could no longer resist. Harvard picked up the journal just to read that single entry.

~ ~ ~

7/31/20—

　　There was not a single notable thing that happened today, so this entry may be shorter than usual. Today I traded a packet of Skittles I got in an MRE for a chocolate chip cookie. I ate the cookie and did not share with anyone. Nobody must know I had the cookie, they will become super jealous and sad and that would be bad. Other than this, there is nothing else to report. My plan for tomorrow is to trade the Snickex bar from the MRE for a sugar cookie and a carton of milk. Once again I shall not share the cookie in order to make sure people aren't sad.

Harvard was really nice today. He let me play with Ranger all day long and even gave me a tennis ball to toss around with him. I wonder what he thinks of all this. He's a dog, does he even understand the concepts of good and evil? Does he even understand the concept of war? He's not motivated to fight like I am—his parents weren't gassed when he was young. Speaking of which, I really should invest in a psychiatrist.

He's not a fighter by any means. Honestly he's a squish ball of goo and love. I don't think he's capable of murder. But if he was, and let's suppose he is for this thought experiment, what would his thought process be? Would it be, "I see an enemy soldier, I need to kill him," or "This is a man who wants to hurt me, I need to kill him," or is it, "That man wants to hurt my team. I must kill him to protect my friends,"? I suppose I'll never get the answer to this. I know what my thought process would be—not that I want to shoot anyone.

~ ~ ~

Harvard closed the journal. "Wow." He muttered, then promptly returned it to it's spot on the duffle bag. With that, he crawled into his bed and stared at the bunk above him for a while, simply letting his mind wander and eyelids grow heavier.

Seemingly, all he did was blink and it was suddenly 05:30. "What?" He whispered to himself, confused as could be. It was light out now, and Harvard never even remembered falling asleep. He came up with two logical conclusions: time travel accident, or alien abduction. It made perfect sense. Still, he felt well rested, so there was no sense in complaining about it.

Slowly, he climbed out of bed and grabbed a fresh ACU from his duffle bag and quietly changed uniforms. He zipped up his boots and crept out of the CHU and onto the airfield. Standing out in the open was First Lieutenant Paul talking to Second Lieutenant Stern. Instantly the two officers turned to face Harvard.

"Good morning, sir." Harvard saluted Paul, making a point not to address Stern. Paul smiled and returned the salute, whereas Stern simply rolled his eyes.

"Morning, Harvard." he replied.

"Hey, you know that this soldier misbehaves and is disrespectful?" Stern pointed at Harvard with a bladed hand. Paul just rolled his eyes.

"It's part of his charm." Paul smiled, "But in all seriousness, he's a damn fine soldier and gets more done in a day than most of your guys do in a week. You have a problem with a go getter? Fine. But let me command my soldiers the way I like. I don't bitch at you for commanding yours, do I?" His smile shifted to a sly smirk. Harvard chuckled quietly to himself.

Stern grunted, "Well, Private First Class Reginald Harvard of Alpha Platoon, I'm certain your enlisted brain won't understand me if I don't explain this in simple terms." Harvard's hands formed loose fists, "We are all eating morning food in the DFAC together today to talk about a plan to retake a few strategic—oh perhaps that's too big of a word—important towns east of the airfield." The Second Lieutenant took extra care to make sure he sounded as condescending as possible.

"Go fuck yourself, Stern. Harvard's smarter than you." Paul growled.

"No way, he's an enlisted man." Stern snarled.

"Watch. I'll prove it." He smirked, "What are the zeroes of the quadratic 'y equals twelve X squared plus twenty X plus three'?"

Stern stared at Paul with a stupid look on his face for a while before replying with a simple, "I don't know."

"That's what I thought. Harvard?"

"Negative .3 repeating and negative .5." Harvard smirked.

Stern's gaze fell on Paul, "Is that correct?"

"Probably." Harvard's answer was not correct.

"Oh well that's just math, anyone with a calculator can do that." Stern spat, not willing to admit defeat. "Where was the treaty of Versailles signed?"

Harvard's palm hit his face with an audible smack. "You gotta be fucking kidding me, did you even take World History? Versailles, France. It was signed on the 28th of June, 1919. Anyone with half a brain can answer that." Stern turned to face Paul.

"See, I told you he was disrespectful." Stern told him.

"Whatever." Paul shifted his attention to Harvard, "Company breakfast at 07:00. I need to get our mission from Captain Levi so I may be a tad late. Dismissed." Harvard snapped to a salute, prompting a more relaxed return from his commander. With that, Harvard began wandering towards the DFAC for a morning cup of coffee."

~ ~ ~

Time passed, as it must, and all Harvard did for the past hour was lean against the walls of the DFAC sipping on his cup of jet black coffee. The desert sun had yet to plunge the airfield into the typical hell, and was actually quite pleasant at the time.

At 06:56, Harvard finally walked into the DFAC to assume his position at the normal table. He wasn't hungry in the slightest, so he didn't bother wading through the line of soldiers that nearly spilled out the front door. Eventually Herbert and Carl joined him, already conversing about something Harvard didn't care about.

Eventually Abram, Paul, and Fern sat down at the table. Fern was carrying his mountain of breakfast along with Paul's omelet while the Lieutenant held a noticeably thick manilla folder. "Alright folks, we've got a special task for today." Harvard felt a bit sick at the words "special task"; that never meant anything good. "It's actually quite awesome, because I get to come too." Paul announced, a stupid smile on his face. At that point, Harvard was very worried as he never liked taking Paul with him on operations. Usually Paul would complain about the heat, or that he was tired from marching, or that his backpack was too heavy, and someone would end up carrying Paul's stuff: usually Harvard.

"What are we doing, sir?" Carl asked with his typical southern charm and impeccable smile. At that moment Harvard decided that the Texan would be the one to carry Paul's backpack when he inevitably got tired.

"Oh I'm so glad you asked!" Abram rolled his eyes.

"You're gonna be sorely disappointed..." Abram grumbled.

"Shush!" Paul couldn't help smiling, "We're running reconnaissance!" Harvard put his hand on his sidearm contemplating if he should shoot himself. His logic was if he shot himself in the foot, he wouldn't have to babysit Paul during a recon mission. "In a bar in Gamarra." Paul finished.

At once, Harvard started grinning like a madman. He took his hand off his sidearm and placed it flat on the table. "Recon in a bar. Serious information gathering, just like university." he laughed at his own joke.

"For the love of fuck, Harvard, it's called college." Abram grunted.

"Fuck off."

"Are we marching or driving?" Herbert asked.

Paul leaned back in his chair as best as he could. "Do you think I want to walk in *that* weather?" He pointed out the window at the now fully lit airfield, "We're driving in an open humvee with a mounted M2. Is gonna be so frickin' cool!"

"Awesome." Carl was as giddy as a puppy awaiting a treat.

"Oh, Harvard, Staff Sarge Webb needs Ranger. Their EOD sniffer got shot yesterday." Paul reported prompting an immediate surge in adrenaline.

"Holy shit is he okay?" Harvard then began thinking about what could happen to *his* dog.

Paul put his hands behind his head, still leaning in his chair, "Yeah he's fine, went straight through his leg. Five-five-six FMJ, nothing serious. He'll be up in a month or so." Paul's eyes met Harvard's seeing the evident distress on his face. "They're just doing a patrol around base, he'll be perfectly safe." Harvard let a sigh of relief escape his lungs.

Fern, through a food stuffed mouth, asked, "So did you just get us this so we could drink?"

"Heavens no!" Paul shot up in his chair, "Actually we're not even allowed to drink. Norton wants us to keep an eye on the locals because he's worried they'll start to be uncooperative with our men." Both Herbert and Harvard groaned in perfect unison.

"Next you'll tell us we need to carry weapons." Herbert grumbled.

"Oh yeah, full kit."

"*Fuck!*" Herbert shouted with such vigor and volume that the table next to them started staring.

"One of these days, you better learn to shut your stupid fucking mouth." Harvard groaned. "We dismissed, sir?"

"Yeah go do what you gotta do." Paul waved his hand, signaling that the men were free to move.

~ ~ ~

At 09:37 the men finally arrived at the same parking lot in Gamarra from a week prior. Nothing had changed—it was still the same disgusting lot with the same bored soldiers standing guard, the same run down headquarters building, and the same nameless crowds of civilians wandering aimlessly. Never before had these familiar surroundings send a shiver down Harvard's spine.

Thankfully, the mission was fairly straightforward. All they had to do was sit around in the pub for roughly three hours to keep an eye on any civilians that seemed suspicious. Since Abram had managed to convince Paul to allow the men to have one drink, it should be pretty enjoyable. "Famous last words." Harvard smirked. His mind returned to the first thing his Senior Drill Instructor ever said during basic training: "If it can go wrong, it will go wrong, I guarantee it." This sentence was followed by a five mile run and sixty pushups, but still the message was the same.

As soon as the men entered the bar, they found the nearest empty table and sat down. It was so strikingly familiar to the

DFAC setup that it was almost humorous. All around them empty old wooden tables scattered the establishment with only a few people here and there to occupy them. Abram elbowed Harvard in the shoulder, "You're taking drink order. Get me a neat whisky, and not the shitty kind."

Harvard furrowed his eyebrows, "Do they even have whisky here?"

"I've been in this fucking desert since you first learned to masturbate, I think I would know if they had whisky." He grumbled. "And make sure it ain't shit."

"Yes sergeant." He sighed and addressed the rest of the unit, "Okay assholes, what'll it be?"

"A tall glass o' strawberry vodka." Fern giggled, "And get a can of pineapple juice, and an apple."

"What the fuck, dude?" Herbert squinted at the private, his mouth slightly ajar exposing yellowing front teeth. "Whatever, just a beer for me."

"I'll take a neat whisky too." Paul smiled warmly, "Why not, right? Special occasion." Harvard couldn't help but smile along with his lieutenant.

"A glass of milk for me, Harv." Abram bursted into a fit of laughter immediately. He nearly fell out of his seat and needed to brace himself on the table with his hand.

"No no no. You're getting him a shot of tequila." The sergeant produced a toothy, malicious grin. Carl raised his hand to protest, but Abram pushed it back down, "No if ands or buts, this goody-two-shoes is gettin' hammered."

"But sergeant I—"

"What part of 'no if ands or buts' didn't you understand?"

"Sarge, it's kinda hard to dip a cookie in a shot of tequila." Harvard couldn't help but smile.

"You two are fucking gay. Harvard, please tell me you've got some sense. What're you gettin'?" Abram leaned back in his seat with his hands behind his head.

"Bourbon if they have any. Otherwise I may join Herbert and crack open a cold one." He stood up and scanned the room to find that another man had entered the bar—he looked about nineteen years old, dark tan skin, a long scabbed over slash crossed his left cheek. He wore a black jacket that was covered in dirt stains blotching his chest and sleeves. His trousers were an old pair of M81 woodland camouflage; torn at the knees and tattered at the heels like they had gotten caught underneath his shoes and had been grinder in the dirt. His boots were once coyote tan, but were now almost brown with perhaps years of neglect. Both he and Harvard refused to make eye contact with each other.

Harvard made his way to the bartender to retrieve his squad's drinks. He leaned against the bar in such a way as to keep the man in the jacket in his peripheral vision at all times. "English?" Harvard asked. The bartender simple nodded as he leaned in like he was about to tell Harvard a secret. "Okay. I need a beer, the shittiest you can find, two glasses of whisky, neat, the finest you have, a glass of milk... actually put some vodka in that milk." A smirk crept onto the soldier's lips, "Neat bourbon if you've got any," the bartender nodded once more, "And..." Harvard sighed, "A tall glass of strawberry vodka—I can't believe I'm doing this—a can of pineapple juice, and an orange." The bartender raised an eyebrow, "Yeah I know he's a fucking moron."

The bartender disappeared into a trance as he began to prepare the drinks, opening bottles and pouring various liquids.

Two more men entered the bar, both of them were dressed in filthy red jumpsuits with matching hardhats in color and cleanliness. The Birkinistani Relief Project's insignia was plastered onto their left shoulders. Harvard groaned at the sight, "Liberal pussies..." He shot a glance at his sergeant who had also noticed the two relief workers. They were as tan as the locals, but were obviously American evident by their high quality boots and expensive watches. "Expensive", in this case, was relative to what the typical Birkinistani local could afford.

    Without saying a word, the bartender set the drinks on a black plastic tray in front of Harvard. A small white slip of paper had "$23.99" scribbled on it in red permanent marker. "I'll pay you when we leave." Harvard said as he scooped up the tray. The bartender simply nodded in reply.

    He returned to the table with the drinks in hand, distributing them to his friends with respect to their orders. Upon completion he flopped into his chair with a grunt and the tiniest sip of bourbon. "This tastes like ass." Harvard immediately pushed the glass away from him.

    "You try putting a drop of water in it?" Paul asked.

    "Uh... no." Harvard rested his cheek into his fist, "Wouldn't that just water it down?"

    "Nope. The oils will react with the water and..." the lieutenant trailed off as his eyes fell upon Abram. The sergeant had three 600mg pills of ibuprofen in one hand and the glass of whisky in the other. Without any hint of apprehension, he popped the three pills into his mouth and downed the entire glass of whisky in a single swig.

    He gently placed the glass back down on the table, "This shit tastes like fuck." It seemed that only Paul and Harvard had noticed

Abram's display of complete disregard for his liver, as they were the only two staring at the sergeant wide eyed and mouths ajar. "Fuck's wrong with you two?"

"Did you just…" Paul bit his bottom lip and broke his gaze on the sergeant.

"Fuck's wrong with us? Fuck's wrong with *you*? You're going to get liver cancer, I guarantee it." Harvard sighed and slouched back in his chair. There was no way he was going to finish that bourbon. "This shit tastes like sewer water that was fermented in someone's asshole."

It felt like a few hours had passed with nothing but a few conversations happening here and there, people coming and going from the bar, and nothing interesting even happening. Harvard had finally admitted it to himself: war was boring.

Herbert and Fern were talking relatively quietly with each other. Herbert flicked a bottle cap back and forth between his hands, "Yeah I guess I just don't recognize it." He told him, "Civilians will be civilians. They're fucking morons."

"It's like that's all they see in us." Fern ran his fingers through his unkempt hair, "Are we just not even people anymore?"

"Right?" Herbert rested his nose on his wrist, "We're just… I dunno, uh…" He picked his head up to snap his fingers a few times, "Secondary?"

"Not secondary. They put the refugees ahead of us." Fern stared off into space, "We're almost not even people to them…" He looked down at the table, "We *aren't* people to them."

"Are we even people to the army?" Herbert made direct eye contact with Fern.

"Perhaps not." Fern sighed, "Weird, ain't it? It's all the civilians see and the army refuses to see it."

"See what?" Carl asked innocently.

Both Fern and Herbert said different things in unison. Herbert replied with, "Killing," and Fern replied with, "PTSD." They both glared at each other, seemingly unaware that the whole time they were talking they had been referencing different things. Abram grunted and sipped on a glass of water.

"You know that's not real, right?" Herbert slouched back in his seat, not taking his eyes off Fern. He returned the specialist's gaze with the most serious glare Harvard had ever witnessed.

Through grit teeth Fern replied with, "Well I guess we'll just have to disagree on that then."

"I'm…" Harvard slowly stood up and picked up his rifle, "Going to go piss." He checked back to see that the two were still staring and allowing their anger to fester before promptly vacating the vicinity.

On his way into the restroom he bumped into one of the men in the red jumpsuits. They exchanged glares and eye rolls as Harvard moved past him into the latrine. One whiff from the room was enough to burn his nose hairs off and melt his eyes. It was comparable to the Germans' mustard gas in the trenches during the First World War, and just as horrifying as a sarin attack in the Southern Province. Still, he did what he needed to do. He found the nearest open stall and shut the door behind him. That was when he realized that the source of the stench was that the building lacked a sewage system. These toilets were nothing more than white porcelain thrones sitting above a massive hole dug only about fifteen feet deep. Even in the dim lighting conditions, Harvard could easily see the mountain of feces that lay at the bottom of the chasm, along with needles and other drug paraphernalia. There even appeared to be a rusty handgun sitting muzzle up sticking out of a mound of feces.

He relieved himself quietly with a grimace. His urine stream disturbed the fecal matter, convincing new putrid particles to fly free from their resting positions and into the air for Harvard to inhale. He coughed and gagged as he buttoned his trousers.

Some yelling erupted from the main tavern. It was undecipherable as the walls muffled any coherence that may have been present. He figured it was probably only a few drunken men screaming because they were intoxicated, but the screaming persisted. Soon enough the familiar booming voice of his platoon sergeant bursted through the walls, "Drop the fucking gun!"

"Oh shit!" Harvard didn't even bother with the top button of his trousers or his belt. He unslung his rifle and rushed out the door as fast as he possibly could, muzzle pointed right in front of him, finger on the safety ready to disengage at any moment.

The tavern was in absolute anarchy. The bartender had a massive slash across his face, blood dripping down his arm as he attempted to stop the bleeding with a white raggedy towel. A civilian in a white polo was on the floor with what appeared to be a smashed beer bottle laying next to him. One of the two relief workers was performing CPR on him while the other was holding a flipped over table as an improvised (and completely useless) form of cover. All through this a few civilians panicked as they ran from end to end for reasons unknown.

Harvard's eyes flew to his friends who had apparently taken defensive positions in the far corner of the bar, rifles pointed outward ready to fire. "One, two, three, four... four..." Harvard counted. "Fuck." He took his rifle off safe and started scanning the room, trying to focus in through the screaming to see if he could find any indication of a threat.

He couldn't seem to find the source of the panic anywhere. "Perhaps it's them?" Harvard thought. It was a plausible theory, he didn't see any other armed individual in the tavern. Had someone completely lost their mind and pulled a gun on a civilian, the ensuing judicial fallout would destroy what little respect Alpha Platoon had in the first place. "Drop the fucking gun or we will fire!" Abram's voice shattered the illusion in an instant—and that's where Harvard figured it out.

Standing about five yards from the mess of soldiers huddled in the corner was unmistakably Carl, trembling like a leaf in a hurricane, his fingers locked together with his hands behind his head—the universal gesture of surrender. A fire started burning in Harvard's stomach right there, "That damn Texan..." Of all the members of his friend circle, he never in a million years expected Carl to be the one to pull a gun on a friendly, let alone civilians. He flicked the safety off, and aligned his red dot sight right on Carl's head. If someone didn't come to apprehend him, Harvard was going to end him right there.

"This is your last chance! Drop the weapon!" Paul shouted, his M9 visibly shaking in his hands.

"What the hell?" Harvard took his eyes off his rifle and searched the immediate area around Carl for anything. There was a woman crying in the corner of the room, dressed in a traditional burka, a boy standing on a table, a few smashed glasses and bottles, and the aforementioned relief workers. Upon the realization that there was a boy standing on a table, he snapped his head back to see that this boy in a black shirt had a handgun pointed at Carl's temple.

With a quick readjustment of his rifle, the red dot was placed on the back of the boy's head right at the base of the skull. Harvard's eyes met his lieutenant's, who nodded discreetly—a silent order for him to do his job; so he did. He snapped his eyes back to his target, and squeezed the trigger.

CHAPTER 7 - PAUL

He blinked. That was all it took to spare him from watching the moment of impact. His new field of vision showed him little more than a blood splatter against the opposite wall, a hole the size of a dime punched through it giving way to the sunlight outside. The particles of dust and smoke danced through the beam of light—a ballet of ghosts to the ballad of tinnitus. They danced upon a stage decayed by time in a theater of crimson.

Quickly Harvard lowered his rifle and engaged the safety, muzzle pointed at the ground, finger off the trigger. He took a deep breath through his nose, the metallic scent of blood mixed with the unmistakable pungent odor of burned gunpowder. "You good?" Harvard asked, not sure if he was talking to Carl or himself. The Texan nodded weakly.

"Harvard, get your ass over here right now." Abram growled, his distinct animalistic voice came from behind the ruined table to the front. He let his boots do the walking until he was right beside his sergeant. He kept his eyes forward not unlike he was at attention. "Look."

"No, sergeant."

"I said look, fucker. You don't get to say no." His hand grasped the back of Harvard's head and forced him to gaze into the gaping hole that used to be the boy's face. Pink mush spilled from the cavity, mixing with blood and dust. His nose was gone, replaced by a typical exit hole of a 7.62 millimeter bullet. One eye had been torn to shreds, the other sat staring upward directly in Harvard's still in it's socket in near perfect condition. Every swirl of brown and gold in that eye was clear as day, yet it was empty. It no longer felt like a human being's eye, but rather a doll's—plastic, unfeeling, dead. That's precisely what the boy was: dead.

"What the fuck is this?" He raised the boy's weapon in front of Harvard's face, obscuring the mess of gore for a moment, snapping him back to reality.

"That's his handgun." Harvard's voice became little more than a whisper.

"Do handguns use CO2 cartridges?" He ripped the back of the weapon off to expose a shiny metallic tube with the words "compressed gas" written in black ink etched on the side. His heart sank to his knees. "This counts as a war crime, Harvard. You shot an unarmed kid!"

"You saw him!" Harvard shouted as loud as he possibly could, "There was no way I could've possibly known that!" He dropped his rifle and allowed it to clank against the ground, letting his hands form fists to prepare himself to punch his sergeant in the face at any moment. "You would've done the exact same thing!" His face contorted into an indescribable mess of anger, hatred, disgust, fear, he didn't even know at this point.

"There's no denying that I wouldn't have." Abram dropped the boy's weapon on the ground. Harvard released tension on his fists. "You still fucked up beyond all repair, and because of that, we *all* fucked up beyond all repair."

"No no." One of the relief workers spoke, "Just him." He pointed at the civilian he had been preforming CPR on. "He's on you too, by the way." He promptly began walking out of the bar.

"Way-to keep our nation safe, *Harvard*." The other sneered, "You're a *real hero*." The other followed close behind his friend.

"Don't bother, they're not worth it." Paul put his hand on Harvard's shoulder. "I'll see what I can do on the legal front, but you know those two are going to cause a mess with the media."

"Fuckin' liberals." Abram grunted, "We're on your side. We were all here to see it happen. You ain't going through this alone." Abram picked up Harvard's rifle and slung it over his shoulder.

~ ~ ~

The next few hours were a blur. One minute Harvard was riding in the back of a Military Police HMMWV, the next he was in a holding cell back at Ulysses. He still heard the damned ringing, which seemed to echo off of the grey concrete walls of his cell.

He was alone in the cell, and in fact the entire tiny detention center was empty as well. He was in complete and utter isolation. He simply sat on the small single mattress placed on the floor of the cell, his back propped up against the back wall.

His mind wasn't wandering, though he stared off into space, replaying the events of the pub over and over again, trying to think of what he could've done differently to perhaps defuse the situation. Harvard wondered if the boy even knew his weapon was nothing more than a BB gun. He assumed that he did, given that he never did attempt to fire the weapon at any point. "Did he just do it to prove a point?" He asked the silence, receiving no answer or reconciliation.

"What was his name?" Another question that would forever go unanswered. There would be no funeral for him, no eulogy, not even a moment of silence in his honor. He will forever be remembered as nothing more than the Boy in the Black Shirt. Nothing more, nothing less, nothing forever.

An MP appeared from down the hall, "You ready?" She asked. Harvard simply nodded his head. "Alright. Follow me." She flipped a switch on the side of the cell to disengage the magnetic locks, then pushed the cell door open. The detention block blurred past like the ride there, he didn't take in any details whatsoever, just that he was moving. The boy in the black shirt wouldn't get to move again.

When Harvard came to, he found himself sitting in between Second Lieutenant Stern and First Lieutenant Paul at a desk. Across from him was Captain Porfiry, the commander of the Military Policy on Ulysses. Nobody said anything for a little while.

"You feeling okay?" Paul asked to break the silence. Harvard still said nothing. Paul sighed and looked to Porfiry. "He's still shaken up from the whole ordeal." Porfiry gave a single nod in understanding.

"That's alright. Harvard, do you know everyone in the room? I want you to feel comfortable for this." Porfiry asked. Harvard looked around the office, not taking note of the organized layout or anything, but simply observing the people. He locked eyes with Stern for a brief moment, but long enough for him to see the disgusting grin on the officer's face.

"Yes, sir." Harvard said weakly.

"Glad to hear, private. Would you like anything to drink? Water, soda, uh... flavored watery beverages?" Porfiry reached down into what appeared to be a small cooler beneath his desk.

"Now hold on, sir. Let's not forget why we're here. Harvard, you shot an unarmed civilian today." Second Lieutenant Stern announced.

"Just one second, Stern," Paul snapped, "Civilian yes. Unarmed no. The boy was holding a weapon that looked real enough to be mistaken for a firearm. He had every right to be confused."

Stern rolled his eyes and replied, "That may be the case, but as a soldier it's his job to identify real threats and avoid civilian casualties. He should've been able to ID the weapon as fake."

"That's not fair." Paul glared at Stern.

"I disagree. I took the liberty of looking through his review board notes from his last promotion, and I found something interesting." Stern flicked his thumb over the side of a manilla folder that appeared to be Harvard's personnel file, "He claims that he is a top tier soldier with, and I quote, 'an intimate know-how of the military structure, history, and materiél.' Tell me, does that sound like the kind of person who would mistake a BB gun for a pistol?" Paul watched the color drain from his soldier's face.

"That's completely unfair and irrelevant. If police officers back in the states make the same mistakes—with more training regarding these kinds of situations mind you—then a soldier who's purpose is to shoot terrorists certainly can too." Paul spat, particles of saliva that was propelled by the sheer intensity of his words flew onto Harvard's face. He simply ignored it, too conflicted and ashamed to do anything.

"Doesn't matter. We're better than that, or at least we're supposed to be. Oh! And let us not forget *who* Harvard shot: a civilian child. A poor innocent boy with so much to live for, crushed under the American boot. You see Harvard? You're the reason the people back in America hate the armed forces. To them, we're all just heartless murderers—baby killers. And you doing shit like this adds more fuel to the fire." Stern scolded. Harvard tightened his fist as much as he could, wishing he could punch Stern in his mouth, or eye, or nose. The private let his rage fester.

"Was he supposed to let Carl die?" Paul asked.

"Private Darling, would not have died because it was a fake weapon." Stern slouched back in his chair with a sly grin on his face.

"Let me stop you two right here." Captain Porfiry's voice was oddly soothing, "It's obvious that Harvard didn't know that the weapon was fake. If he did I'm certain he would've attempted to apprehend the boy instead of killing him." Both Paul and Stern took a moment to think about what he had just said before continuing their debate.

"Are you certain of that?" Stern asked.

"Positive." Porfiry's eyes fell on Harvard before repeating more softly, "Positive."

The second lieutenant sighed, "Well let me remind you about civilian mainstream media. What have they been broadcasting recently?" Stern paused before continuing, "Police brutality on blacks, and collateral damage on civilians."

"Oh here we go again…" Paul rolled his eyes.

"It's quite simple really. Even if Harvard knew the boy's weapon was fake, are we certain that a white male would've been so kind as to simply 'apprehend' a muslim child? I don't think so. I believe that Harvard may have shot the boy simply because he is racist towards muslims, and had he been say… a white boy pointing a gun to Carl's head, he would've attempted to apprehend him." Stern smirked.

"Second Lieutenant Stern, what the fuck is wrong with you? Your argument has no logic to it at all, you're just calling him racist on the grounds that he shot someone with a gun." Paul focused his gaze on Porfiry, "Are you really going to let him get away with this?"

"But does it make sense? Look at him! He's a gun wielding, disrespectful, privileged, white male from a conservative family." His sly grin morphed into a malicious smile, "Besides, the Birkinistani Relief Project workers reported that Harvard executed the boy without even talking to him first. No attempts were made to quell the situation, just *bang!* And he was dead." Harvard's fist began shaking from holding it so tight. "Are we just going to throw due process out the window with this one? If we will with him, shouldn't we with Harvard?"

"That's ridiculous and you know it. Harvard is the most tolerant person I know. Even more than me." Paul barked.

"Well, Paul, I am going to have to tell you that the ROE in civilian towns is 'do not fire unless fired upon'. He didn't necessarily follow them." Porfiry said casually. "Granted, given the circumstances there wasn't much of a choice he had."

"I know that." Paul sighed, "I told him to fire." Harvard couldn't remember if he received the order or not.

"No you didn't." Stern paused, "I know you, Paul. Taking the bullet for someone else, *how selfless*." His sarcastic tone boiled Harvard's blood. "But no. I think I've known you long enough to know your little game."

"What game?" Paul furrowed his brow.

"The 'look good in front of superiors so I can get promotions and more money' game."

"Fuck off!" Paul shouted, "You know what?! Yeah! I do try to look good in front of my commanders. I *do* try to get promotions and commendations. But you know what I do more?" He paused, perhaps for dramatic effect, perhaps he really wanted an answer. It didn't matter, "I try to look good in front of my men, because *they're* the ones who go and fight. *They're* the ones who get paid dirt for doing *our* jobs, and if I'm going to condemn them to death, then I'm sure as hell going with them." Paul boiled for a moment then slammed his fist on the desk to the surprise of Porfiry, "I haven't *once* seen you on combat patrol! And when you do leave the comfort of your cubicle, you're at a FOB, or field HQ, or 'on leave', eating three hot meals a day, hot showers, cozy bed, clean as a whistle." He paused, "But I'm out there with *my* men in the dirt and mud, cooking MREs in a ditch, listening to mortars landing not even half a klick away. I'm *better* than you. You're nothing."

"Doesn't fucking matter. This isn't about *you* or me." Stern focused his attention on Harvard once more, "This is about him— once again demonstrating to the public that the American military is nothing more than a band of murderers, rapists, pedophiles, et cetera. Great job, Harvard. You're a real he—"

"What was his name?" Harvard interrupted Stern. There was a different sort of silence that fell over the room. The others were an awkward silence, a silence of not knowing what to say. This was a dead silence, as if all the life in the room had been drained by Harvard's words.

"What?" Stern asked.

"The boy. What was his name?" Harvard's fists shook even more from the tight balls they were clenched in.

"I..." Stern trailed off, "I don't know..." Harvard turned to Paul who shook his head, then to Porfiry who refused to make eye contact.

"Right. That's exactly what I thought. You don't know. You don't care to know." Harvard stared at Stern right in the eyes. "You don't care about him. The only reason you care about this at all is because you finally have a chance to get me out of your life forever. You never liked me because I don't respect the douche bag that you are. You hate me, and I hate you. This isn't about justice, this is about hurting me. Within yourself you know that there was no way I could've known the weapon was fake, you know I'm not racist, you know I am not a murderer. But you justify me as such so that you don't feel bad when I get dishonorably discharged or sentenced to death by the UN. You don't care that the boy that I shot will never rest in peace, because we don't even know his name. We never will know his name. He's just another face in a mass grave. You don't see the enemy as a person. You see him as that: the enemy. You've never had to kill anyone before." Harvard felt a tear fall from his eye and down his cheek. "But you know how I really know you don't care? You never once told me about Carl."

The dead silence returned. The room felt as though it had become colder, like the ghost of the boy in the black shirt had joined in on this conversation. Perhaps he did. Perhaps the boy was watching and waiting for Harvard to be ordered to the court martial.

"Private Carl Darling is alright." Porfiry told him, cracking a smile on Harvard's otherwise stone face. Paul put his hand on Harvard's shoulder.

"I took care of him. He's back at the CHU playing with Ranger. He's a little bit shaken up, but he's alright." Paul said reassuringly, genuine care in his voice.

Stern still said nothing. He appeared to be speechless, like Harvard had completely destroyed his entire argument. His eyes bled hatred as they bored into his skull, seeming to whisper "I hate you, private." without a single word leaving his mouth.

"Well, I think I've heard enough to make my decision. First Lieutenant Paul, I recommend that you do not issue anything to Harvard, as he was simply doing his job as a United States Soldier. Given the situation, I would've done the same. Of course, the ultimate decision is up to you being his commander. Though I'm certain I already know how you would like to proceed." Porfiry picked up a pile of papers on his desk, and straightened them with a single click on his desk before setting them back down flat.

"Yeah. I'm not issuing any citation. Private Reginald Harvard shall not be sent to the court martial." First Lieutenant Paul told Porfiry.

"Private Reginald Harvard shall not be sent to the court martial." Captain Porfiry repeated. Stern grunted in dismay, prompting Paul to glare at him. Porfiry clicked a pen on the table, then flipped it over so that he could write something on some forms in front of him. He clicked the pen once again, and handed the forms to Paul. His gaze fell upon Harvard once again. "Well, you're a free man. Do you have anything you want me to do for you right now?"

There was another silence that lasted for a few minutes, before Harvard replied, trying his best not to cry. "Sir, I just want to go home."

CHAPTER 8 - WYSTAN

It had been about a week since the incident in the pub, and Harvard had managed to convince his superiors that he was perfectly fine. Truthfully, however, he had spent every night dreaming of the boy in the black shirt. Sometimes the boy would speak to him, sometimes it was a simple replay of the events, sometimes he was in complete control and tried to save Carl, only to find the weapon was real. Those were the worst nights.

"Harvard, front and center!" Abram shouted, prompting Harvard to fall in in front of the Master Sergeant.

"Sergeant, Private First Class Reginald Harvard reports as ordered!" Harvard sounded off with a salute, trying his best to keep a straight face. Abram furrowed his brow, not expecting a formal report.

He returned the salute, then dropped it prompting Harvard to drop his. "Uh… okay. At ease." Harvard shifted to rest position. "Son, I'm sure you know who Second Lieutenant Stern is. Well that asshole just got Cap'n Levi to volunteer us to assist in a raid on a camel-fucker town in the middle of dick-shit nowhere. We move at 15:30, so be prepared." Harvard silently listened. "So, uh, yeah.

That's how we get to spend our afternoon. Raiding diaper-heads in the desert. Also we're going to be the first ones going in, so we might die. Just letting you know."

"What?" Harvard asked.

"You are at the position of at ease which means that you are not allowed to speak unless otherwise told to!" Abram shouted, then paused, "Nah, just fucking with you. But seriously this is gonna fucking suck, not gonna lie. At least we're not in his platoon, that'd be a death sentence for both us." Abram sighed.

"You think maybe he's trying to kill me?" Harvard gave a lighthearted chuckle.

"Probably. Stern hates you more than a skank hates hard work, especially after the shit you did in Porfiry's office, calling him out like that. Heh, wish I could'a seen it." He smiled, "So yeah I can see why he wants us in first." He chuckled, "Does seem like a lot of work to kill just one person."

Harvard sighed, thinking about the boy a bit, then about how much he wanted to punch Stern in the mouth. "Doesn't Paul have anything he can do about this? I mean *he's* our commander, not Stern. Seems weird that he has the authority to voluntell us." He leaned to the side to relieve his weight off his right foot.

"Yeah you'd think that'd be the case, but nope. Paul can't do shit. It's an order coming from Captain Levi, not the lieutenants. Trying to do anything about it'll be like arguing with an SJW on Tumblr..." Abram paused, "Fuckin' hate Tumblr. That's besides the point though. Also, Herbert got discharged."

Harvard gave Abram a surprised look, "Discharge? For what?"

"Claimed PTSD, got the doc to sign a form. He just flew out like an hour ago. Just poof, gone. Like a fucking fairy." Abram looked off in the distance, "Damn pussy."

"Sergeant, is that all?" Harvard asked.

"Yeah get the fuck out of my face." Abram ordered. Harvard snapped to attention and saluted Abram, who returned the salute. Harvard took a step backwards out of formation then casually walked away towards his CHU to play with Ranger before the raid. It was only 09:54, so he had plenty of time before he would need to report in. He figured that Stern was a lot more serious when it came to mobilizing for the operation, and they would actually have to go through a whole formation instead of just piling into a vehicle like normal. That said, he figured that Stern's annoying antics would be future Harvard's problem. It was time to talk to Carl and play keep away with Ranger.

When he did arrive at his CHU, he found Stern berating Carl for some reason. Harvard slowly walked closer trying to figure out what Stern was so mad about. "When an officer walks by, you are to salute and say 'good morning, sir'! 'Howdy', is not an appropriate greeting!" Stern then forced Carl to salute him over and over again. Even from the distance he was, Harvard could tell that the private was sweating profusely as he preformed the motions repeatedly in the desert heat.

"Good morning, sir." Harvard said as he approached Stern with a salute. Stern turned his head and rolled his eyes as the private's face registered in his mind.

"What do you want, Harvard? Wanting to talk to me about not sending you in first?" Stern taunted.

"No sir. I wanted to remind you that since you were so infuriated with Carl about rendering the proper customs and courtesies that it is customary for you to return the salute that the subordinate renders. So, given that you made Carl salute a good fifteen times, and I saluted you once. You are to salute Carl fifteen times, and me once. Of course, I know you don't want us to be rude to you, I would hope you would want to set a good example for some of the other new privates on base." Harvard smiled and tiled his head like a dog in an attempt to imitate Carl.

"I don't have to salute because I'm an officer." Stern told him before walking away from the scene and towards the offices. Harvard rolled his eyes and looked to his friend.

"Don't let him get to you. He just has a redwood tree growing up his asshole… if that makes sense." Harvard and Carl sat down on the steps with a sleeping Ranger at their feet. The Texan sighed and looked down at the dog, watching the slow rise and fall of his belly.

He reached down and scratched behind Ranger's ear a bit, whispering to him inaudible praises. Ranger really was a great dog. "Well Harvard, he's a total butt wagon." Carl announced, not looking up from the dog. This caused Harvard to fall over laughing hysterically.

"Butt wagon?!" He exclaimed.

"Yeah, butt wagon." Carl smiled still petting Ranger. "He was probably a butt wagon in school, and instead of the red rider for Christmas, he got a butt with wheels on it when he was a kid. I mean, what kind'a guy doesn't like 'howdy'?"

"He's an ass waffle." Harvard smiled.

"A poopie face." Carl added.

"A meanie." Harvard attempted to imitate Carl's childlike southern accent but failing miserably and hilariously at it.

"He's a fart stick." Carl giggled. The two then started laughing like idiots. "Harvard, what are we doing here?" Harvard laughed, thinking the question was rhetorical, but when he looked back at Carl he found that he was no longer smiling. Instead he had his head tilted to the side with the inquisitive eyes of a child.

"Uh..." He paused, "Like, here? On Ulysses?"

"No." Carl sighed, "I mean, what are we doing here in life? Why'd we do this to ourselves?" Something about this question deeply bothered him.

"I..." Harvard paused, "I don't think I have an answer for you." He looked down at Ranger, who was still sound asleep.

Carl sighed deeply, "That's okay." Harvard studied Carl's face, watching him rub the dog's fluff. There was an innocent smile on his face, just a tiny curl of his lips that would go unnoticed by anyone else.

"Carl?"

"Hm?"

"You want a cookie?" He smiled.

"Yes I do."

"Cmon." Harvard stood up, "DFAC time." Carl stood up and nodded, prompting the two men plus Ranger to begin walking towards that wonderful land of free food.

They marched out of step with each other, their boots alternating clicks as they hit the tarmac with the faint sound of Ranger's collar jingling. Off on one end of the runway, and A-10 was making it's way out of it's hanger slowly, engines humming in the distance. The ground crew began hurrying soldiers off the runway in order to clear it for take off.

It wasn't long before Harvard, Carl and Ranger had made it to the DFAC's entrance where they had found Abram arguing with a redhead female soldier. Harvard recognized her instantly and averted his eyes before his face could turn into a tomato. The two were standing underneath an awning as to stay out of the sun that was slowly making it's way over the mountains to scorch the valley that Ulysses sat in. Once the men got close enough, they were able to hear the argument clearly.

"It's called infantry*man* for a reason." Abram scoffed. Harvard felt like someone had punched him in the chest. He had joked many times before about women in the military, but Abram took this topic to the next level. He was scared to see what would happen since he just said such a sexist remark to a female soldier.

"You do realize the Department of Defense is looking to change infantry*man* to infantry*person*, right?" The woman smirked, putting her hands on her hips with as much sass as possible.

Harvard nudged Carl's shoulder with his elbow. "Honestly I don't know why they can't call them infantrywomen." Harvard muttered.

"What about non-binary people?" Carl asked.

"Infantrything. Easy." Harvard chuckled.

Abram stared at her, eyebrows furrowed, head titled to the side ever so slightly, eyes squinted and mouth open just a sliver. "Lady, that's the biggest pile of horse shit on the east side of the Kentucky river!" Abram began sounding off, "There ain't no way in fuck that *my* Army would deface *my* title! Never once have I heard such a lousy way to poke fun at the grunt title! It shall be infantry*man* until the day I die, and it shall be infantry*man* until the end of time!" He bladed his hand and knife handed the woman, his middle finger only inches from her left cheek, "You are a disgrace! The mere fact that you can put on this uniform and call yourself a soldier goes to show that they let any cock sucker in my army. How much dick did you suck in college?" Abram was in her face now.

"None, sergeant. And even if I did, I wouldn't have sucked yours." She smirked an oddly seductively. Harvard couldn't help but let his face turn into a tomato.

"Ooh! You think she's pretty!" Carl exclaimed, a huge smile on his face. The redhead turned her head away from Abram to see Harvard and Carl, and a grin replaced the smirk on her face.

"Carl, you bastard!" He smacked the Texan on the back of the head.

"One moment, sergeant." She winked at Harvard, then turned to face Abram, who practically had steam coming off the top of his head. She deliberately paused for an extended period of time before saying, "Please, continue."

"I assume you just wouldn't be able to handle the sheer magnitude of my penis!" Harvard was certain that this poor girl's eardrums just exploded from the volume. "It is massive, colossal, but I would never fuck a fuckup like yourself because you don't need to get fucked further!" Abram sprayed her with his spit, prompting her to calmly take her hand and wipe it off her face, all not breaking the smirk or eye contact. "You smell of poverty and nicotine, and just by the looks of you, I know that half your kids will die of the plague and the other half will end up a gutter trash in New York! I hope you step on an IED or get fucking shot because you souls ginger fuck will cease to exist! That way, you can't follow me and my men to Hell!"

"Sergeant, I don't think you have much room to talk about hair."

"Gyod-dayum" Harvard whispered.

"It doesn't matter one bit, because the only place suitable for a woman in the military is the kitchen! Now, here is an order coming directly from a noncommissioned officer: Make me a fucking sandwich!" In a blink of an eye, Abram was on the floor with the girl's boot on his chest. The whole thing happened faster than Harvard's brain could register. He couldn't believe his eyes; the same man that he had heard stories of merciless beatings to a Birkinistani soldier, was on the floor with a woman holding him in place. That's not to say it matters that she was a woman, but rather because Abram was Abram.

He was speechless, trying to open his mouth to say something to this girl who had impressed him further than anyone had in his entire life, not to mention that she was probably one of the most beautiful women that Harvard had ever laid eyes on. "Hi." He managed to say. She quickly turned her head from Abram to lock eyes with Harvard, making him jump a bit.

"Hey there." She smiled, a beautiful and warming smile. Any fears of this girl that Harvard previously had were gone, she seemed friendly but certainly like she does not take nonsense from anyone. Her personality made Harvard wonder how she even made it past basic training, not that he cared.

The girl shifted her gaze to Carl, who was grinning like usual. She looked back down at Abram, then stepped off of him with the elegance of a dancer, but the authority of a soldier. She giggled at her defeated foe, then gracefully made her way to Harvard, extending her hand for a handshake. As he reached forward to acknowledge her greeting, she pulled her hand away to form a salute and said, "Private First Class Lilian Wystan reports." Harvard awkwardly returned the salute with a shy, "at ease".

Wystan came to the position of parade rest, then started cracking up at the absurdity of her actions.

"So hey there…" she paused to read his nametape, "Harvard. A little birdie tells me you think I'm pretty."

"Well, um, you see…" An audible groan was heard coming from Abram's mouth. "You uh… took down my sergeant. Gotta say, that's pretty impressive." His heart started racing, sweat forming under his cover.

"Why thank you very much, it was easy. Just a good kick to the nut sack." Harvard felt his cheeks turning red. Abram groaned again. "Lemme know if you need me to do that again."

"Well, uh, I promised this one a cookie." He pointed his thumb at an oblivious Carl who was now focused on a pigeon picking at some fries, "Could I… I dunno… interest you in a cookie too?" Harvard asked, looking down at his boots, kicking a rock back and forth between them nervously.

"Fuckin'… pussy…" Abram groaned.

"Aw, sorry Harvard. I have to report to my unit in like five minutes but certainly some other time." She patted Harvard's shoulder, "Come find me sometime. You know where the cavalry hides." With that, she walked away with a smile on her face.

It seemed like all the tension in his body was released at that moment—the terrifying encounter with the opposite sex was over. Carl appeared next to Harvard. "You gonna go through with her?"

Harvard turned his head to face him, "I… have no idea. Part of me says 'yeah, do it', but another part says 'she's just gonna reject you like everyone else'."

"That's crazy talk. She looks like she's into you… probably." Carl smiled.

"Dude I just… I dunno. Not after high school. No way."
Harvard looked back down at his dirty, mud crusted boots.

"What happened in high school?" Carl asked innocently.

Harvard sighed, "Alexa."

"Who's Alexa?"

"Just someone I used to know." He looked back up at the
Texan, "Come on. Let's get you that cookie."

CHAPTER 9 - ABRAM

"Fall in!" the First Sergeant ordered. He was an African American man that seemingly nobody knew the name of. He was simply known as the First Sergeant, or First Sarge, depending on his mood. His voice echoed across the small empty parking lot the men used as a drill pad. Second Lieutenant Stern had ordered the men to do an actual opening formation, just as anticipated, before moving out to raid the Birkinistani town. Harvard, Fern and Carl stood at attention in that order with Ranger sitting directly to Harvard's front. Abram stood at attention facing his men.

"Report!" Abram shouted, his voice so much louder than Paul's, pounding into Harvard's eardrums. Abram's voice thundered in his chest, rattling his ribs and shaking his lungs. The master sergeant's command voice was perhaps the most terrifying voice that he had ever heard.

At Abram's command, Harvard raised his right hand for a salute. "First squad, all present!" Harvard's sound off was pathetic compared to Abram's jet engine. He raised his right hand for a salute, held it briefly, then brought his hand back down to his side, prompting Harvard to do the same.

The man behind him, who's name Harvard never bothered to learn, sounded off as well. "Second squad, all present!" Even this unknown face behind him had a better sound off than him. Abram saluted the man, then dropped his salute.

Finally, the third squad leader sounded off. "Third squad, all present!" Abram saluted the man, then dropped his salute. The moment his hand returned to his side, Abram's right foot moved to the left side of his other to stand on the toe for a fraction of a second, before spinning on his toes gracefully until his heels met with a click. The standard of what an about face should look like.

He once again saluted and sounded off with, "Alpha platoon, all present are accounted for!" Harvard thanked a God he didn't believe in that the sergeant's maw was pointed away from him this time.

"Bravo platoon, all present are accounted for!" That was the end of the platoon sergeants' yelling for now.

"Ready, post!" The First Sergeant ordered, prompting Captain Levi, a thirty year old brunette lady, to march up to him. The First Sergeant held a salute to her, and shouted, "Ma'am, Phoenix Company all present are accounted for!" She saluted the First Sergeant, held it for a moment, then dropped it, a silent order for the First Sergeant to do the same. The two went to the position of rest, and seemed to begin chatting. Harvard had no idea what they were talking about, not that he really cared. It's not like Levi would be following them into battle. She'd probably just sit in her office, sipping on coffee while her soldiers get killed.

Suddenly, the First Sergeant snapped to attention, saluted her, then walked off the drill pad and onto the airfield. "Platoon commanders take charge of your platoon!" Levi shouted, her voice not nearly as loud as Abram's. Then she walked off the drill pad, never to be seen again.

Paul appeared from out of Harvard's peripheral vision to take his position next to Abram. "On my command, at ease!" He shouted. Instantly, the entire platoon shifted their legs to be shoulder width apart, hands behind their backs bladed and folded together. Some of the men stretched their stiff limbs, others simply sat quietly awaiting their orders.

"Gentlemen," he paused, "This is gonna suck." He paused again, "Like, a lot. A whole lot. But I want to make this clear before we move out: I am so proud to call myself your commander." Harvard tried his best not to groan as he thought about how cliché this speech would be. "For the past year I've been privileged to call myself the commander of Alpha Platoon, and even more privileged to have served alongside you. In my eyes you are all incredible people. I love you... no homo." A small giggle came from the back of the unit, "Now, you're probably wondering why I'm telling you all this now."

"You think we're all gonna die?!" Someone shouted from Second Squad.

"No!" Paul quickly replied, "Heavens no! I wanted to make this announcement now. In five months I'm going to be transferring to Okinawa." Harvard felt his heart rate suddenly spike. "This may be the last time—" someone from Third Squad interrupted him.

"And first!"

"Lock it down!" Abram shouted.

Paul sighed, "...The last time I ever go into battle with you. I wanted to tell you how much this time has meant to me. I've grown a lot as a leader because of you all, and I'm happy to call you my men." Then his eyes fell upon First Squad, "And I'm honored to call some of you my friends." The lieutenant smiled, "Now, on with the program."

"Platoon, ten-*hut*!" Abram ordered. A thump erupted from the platoon as their heels clicked together to snap to the position of attention. There was a brief pause, "Platoon sergeant front and center!" Abram pivoted smartly on his feet, and then marched to his front until he was about one pace away from Lieutenant Paul. They exchanged salutes before moving to "at ease" to discuss the plans for the day. Harvard couldn't hear a word they were saying, nor did he really have decent visuals on the pair. They sat in his peripheral vision, two lumps of green and pink—blobs that were deciding how he was supposed to die.

After some time, the men returned to the position of attention, exchanged salutes, then Abram returned to his post. "Platoon sergeant take command of your platoon!" Paul ordered. Abram and Paul exchanged one final salute before the lieutenant disappeared onto the airfield.

"First squad leader, front and center!" Abram's voice was deafening, but Harvard still felt his legs moving forward to report one pace in front of his sergeant. He was at the position of attention the entire time, not even his eyes moving a tiny bit.

"Sergeant, Private First Class Reginald Harvard reports as ordered." Harvard raised his hand to form a salute, his middle finger touching the brim of his cover. Abram returned the gesture, then dropped his with Harvard following almost immediately after.

"At rest, shit face." He scoffed. Harvard moved to the position of at rest, and let out a yawn. "Well that was gay." Harvard blew a raspberry in an attempt to keep himself from laughing, "Anyways, just in normal army fashion. Guess who's not leaving at 15:30 anymore? That's right, us. Who would'a thunk it, ey?"

"Yeah." Harvard groaned. Abram's face morphed into a look of pure scorn, the poor private immediately regretting his entire life.

"Fuck stain, you are still in formation, you will say 'yes Sergeant', is that understood?" Abram spat.

"Yes Sergeant!" Harvard sounded off.

"Completely just fucking with you. So the actual time this piss brain wants us to move is 16:30, which means we have to stand here for two hours because if you look at your time keeping device, you will see that it is 14:30." Abram paused, "Well, 14:44, so really only an hour and 45 minutes, but that's some shit. Some real fuckery."

"Sergeant, what are you suggesting?" Harvard asked.

"We break some rules, jump the chain of command, go Rambo, if you will." Abram smirked.

"Sergeant, I have a real bad feeling I know what you're about to say." Harvard felt his eyebrows droop down his forehead as his shoulders increased in weight.

"We gonna leave without the other platoon!" Abram exclaimed ecstatically. Harvard groaned.

"Or, how about this? We just, don't go." He smiled.

"Ah don't be such a girl!"

"Might I remind you it was a girl who put you on your ass?"

"Might I remind you to *shut your commie mouth?!*"

"Sergeant, I just don't feel like dying." Harvard shifted his weight to the balls of his feet to take the pressure off his heels.

"Not dying's really easy! I've been in hundreds of firefights and I'm not dead." Abram proudly placed his hands on his hips and puffed his chest.

"No shit."

"The secret to not dying, is to kill them first." His best facsimile of Carl's smile appeared on his face, although his was more creepy than charismatic, "That way they're too dead to kill you!"

Harvard felt his stomach twist and turn as his eyes fell upon Abram's yellow toothed grin, "But I don't want to kill anyone ever again." Flashes of crimson appeared in Harvard's vision, phasing out of existence just as soon as they appeared, "I can't do that again."

The sergeant sighed, "You're an 11b. You kill people. Get over it." Abram scoffed.

"Sergeant, I think I might have PTSD." Abram began laughing hysterically, having to brace himself by placing his hands on his knees.

"Harvard! Buddy! Ya 'lil shit! PTSD isn't real! It's just a ploy made by the liberal media to keep people from joining the military." Abram wiped a tear from his eye caused by his laughter, "All PTSD is, is the brain's inability to move on from something, much like a shitty song getting stuck in your head. You just gotta play that same Justin Bieber song over and over again until it goes away." Abram paused, "What I'm getting at is you need to kill more camel fuckers until you don't feel bad killin' 'em no more."

Harvard was a bit confused, but figured that if his superior was saying it, it must be true. Perhaps PTSD was, in fact, fake, and all he really needed to do was get over himself. Soldiers killed other soldiers, it's what they do. Maybe he really was just being a wimp about the whole thing.

"You're a fucking idiot." Harvard cursed, fire spewing off his lips, "Am I dismissed, *sergeant*?" He made sure to emphasize his superior's title.

He growled, "Yeah. Git yer ass back in formation…" Harvard snapped back to the position of attention, exchanged salutes with Abram, and marched back to his position in line. Abram gazed at his men for a moment, then shouted, "Alright you little shits, you know the drill! Regroup on SL's and do whatever the fuck you're supposed to be doing! If I find anyone *not* doing something, I will fucking murder your asshole with an M60! Di-*smissed!*" On his command, the three squads split off from the formation, the two other squad leaders shouting orders, rushing their men to do whatever it is they were supposed to be doing. First Squad simply followed Abram to the parking lot with all the HMMWVs and trucks.

Their orders were to simple: stand around and not break anything until Paul arrived with the vehicle. Unsure of how long that would take, Harvard tried some conversation.

"Hey Fern, how many classes did you fail when you were in school?" Carl furrowed his brow, probably thinking that such a question was offensive and rude.

"I currently hold my school's record, of eight classes failed in one semester." He paused, "Of six classes." Immediately everyone slowly turned their heads to face Fern, unsure of how to look at him. His tone conveyed that he was oddly proud of the fact he failed this many classes, hence the reason Harvard didn't hesitate to ask the question.

"How, the fuck, do you do that?" Abram asked, completely and utterly astonished.

"Well, I failed all six of my classes, as well as homeroom and lunch." Fern explained, a goofy smile stretched across his face from ear to ear.

"How do you fail homeroom?" Carl asked.

"How do you fail lunch?!" Harvard shouted.

"It's easy to fail homeroom, you just don't show up." He smirked, "Lunch though? That takes some serious talent. Trade secret, my friend."

Harvard had no clue if he should either be impressed with his battle buddy, or appalled. "Just out of curiosity, what were the six subject classes you failed?" He asked.

"Well, I failed biology first period, US history second period, English 11, lunch break which I also proudly failed, Spanish for Spanish speakers, TA for chemistry, and then psychology I." His hands met his hips as he looked off into the distance like a stereotypical superhero.

"If you fail at being a TA, you should kill yourself." Carl's voice was cold, his eyes unfeeling. Harvard turned his head to face him, studying every bit of the Texan's face as he stared into oblivion. Once he noticed his squad leader's gaze, all he gave him was a simple, "What?"

"Nothin'," He shrugged, "Just a bit out of character for you."

"Sorry. I'm just tired." He shifted his gaze to Fern, "Uh... I didn't mean anything by that.

"What? You said something?" It was at that moment that Harvard noticed his red bloodshot eyes.

"Okay then." Carl pressed his lips together and returned to staring off into the distance.

Harvard looked down at Ranger, who was staring back up at him, breathing heavily. Out of boredom, he decided to try something, "Ranger, about face." Harvard ordered. Ranger stood up and spun around, then promptly plopped his butt on the ground. "Ranger, left face." Ranger turned to his left. "Ranger, left right, face." Ranger spun around in a complete circle, causing Harvard to smile a bit. "Ranger, up up down down left right left right B A, face." Ranger sat down and stared up at Harvard for a moment, before flopping on his back with all four of his legs extended in the air. A faint howl escaped his mouth, although it sounded more like he was attempting to sing rather than legitimately howl.

Harvard tried his very hardest not to fall over from the laughter, which was beginning to spread to the other men. This continued for some time without dying down at all as Ranger held the position without breaking the singing noise escaping from his snout. Carl knelt down to rub his belly, prompting the dog to wag his tail uncontrollably. At some point, it seemed like Ranger was attempting to sing a song like "Taps", although if it was "Taps" the tune was unrecognizable and horribly off key. Even still, it was entertainment far better than anything else on base.

Suddenly, an MRAP screeched to a halt in front of the men, and just about a pace from Ranger, who held the position. The door to the vehicle opened and Paul stepped out and just stared at Ranger on the ground. Suppressing his laughter, he managed to let out a pathetic, "That poor dog."

"Holy fuck we got an MRAP!" He exclaimed, a massive smile forming on his face. Ranger quickly stood up in preparation to move out.

"Alright men, get your butts in the truck! We got some dusty nuts to kick!" Paul ordered, prompting the men plus Ranger to load themselves in the MRAP with Harvard taking the driver's seat, Abram on the M2, and Paul in shotgun. Everyone else was in the back Once everyone had buckled themselves in the armored death machine, Paul shouted as loud as he could, "Onward my loyal steed!"

"Sir, I'm not a horse." Harvard replied as he twisted the key in the ignition.

"You're right. You're a goat, which is why only the Birk's'd fuck you." Abram taunted from the back seat.

"Fuck off, Sergeant." Harvard pushed the ignition button began driving towards the front gate of the airfield. Once he arrived, he found that he was behind an HMMWV that decided to leave earlier than the others, and would be taking point in the convoy.

"Wait, Paul you got the weapons right?" Harvard panicked, realizing that his M14 wasn't next to him or slung over his shoulder.

Paul laughed, "I'm not that big of a retard. They're in the back." The private breathed a sigh of relief. The men waited for a long while, as the HMMWV in front didn't seem to move from it's position. Harvard assumed the sentry had left his post in the tiny wooden box.

So they waited, and kept waiting as more and more vehicles moving out to the mission lined behind them until the clock hit 16:30, when the vehicle in front began moving forward, and Harvard about five car's lengths behind. "This entire plan is going to go to shit, I just know it." Paul announced to everyone in the car.

"You think? This is the military, where everything sucks and nothing goes according to plan. Ever." Harvard replied.

"I fucking know that, it's just things are going to get more fucked than normal because Lieutenant Fern I mean Stern, sorry Fern, is in charge of this bullshit." Paul sighed, "Look, I don't expect you all to agree with this mission or anything, but it's necessary. Lot's of innocent people've died." He slouched back in his chair, running his fingers along the seams of his trousers, "Not fair to them."

The droning of the road somehow put both Ranger and Carl to sleep in the back of the MRAP, leaving just Harvard, Paul, Abram and Fern awake. "Hey Paul, pass the aux."

"No your music's trash."

"Fuck you too then."

"Have I ever told you the tale of The Duck?" Fern asked seemingly out of nowhere. The vehicle went silent, as the awake men processed Fern's inquisition.

"Nuts nozzle, what kind of fuck up story is this gonna be?" Just as normal, Abram's voice shattered the sound barrier with the force of a fighter jet. Fern began one of his nonsensical ramblings about how he once got incredibly high and met the most interesting duck in the world. Harvard eventually had enough of Fern's maundering, and took out his standard issue earplugs and flipped them over to the "cancel all" side rather than the "cancel some" side.

He allowed himself to be lost in the road, watching the truck in front of him drive forward on that empty street for what felt like hours. It was quite tranquil. Feeling like he was back in university, Harvard imagined that he was just out on a weekend road trip with his friends to the desert. He pretended that he wasn't a soldier for a little while—nobody was in the desert with a loaded gun ready to kill him, and the only thing that should be on his mind was that the next semester would start in a few weeks, and this was his last chance to have some fun before he had to return to the grind.

That illusion was shattered by a blinding flash, and a deafening bang. The MRAP came to a screeching halt, as did the rest of the convoy behind them. Harvard took out his earplugs and flipped them around then put them back in.

"Sound off!" Paul ordered in his command voice.

"Abram!" The sergeant boomed.

"Darling!"

"Fern!"

"Harvard!"

"Ranger's good too!" Carl reported.

"Harvard, report on vehicle!" Paul ordered. He tried stepping on the gas pedal, but the vehicle just groaned and spewed black smoke out of the engine.

"The damn thing's fucked!" Harvard reported. Paul slammed his fist into the side door.

"God damn it!" He shouted, sighing as he rubbed his forehead. "Abram, stay on the fitty, Harvard check the vehicle outside. Everyone else, stay in the vick."

"Roger." Abram grunted. With that, Harvard drew his M9 from the holster on his hip, and slowly made his way out of the MRAP and onto the road. From a brief look, it appeared as though the M2 machine gun on the vehicle ahead of the men had flown off the rack and lodged itself in the engine block. Perhaps it had discharged a few times while inside the block as well, as there were multiple holes in the vehicle itself with very little evidence to suggest something else had caused them.

In a moment of clarity, or stupidity, or heroism, or selflessness, Harvard turned around and decided to address the damage of the vehicle in front of them. He slowly crept forward more and more as the HMMWV came into view through a cloud of smoke and dust. The chassis was ruined, resembling a piece of metal after a bullet ripped through it. In a strange way, it resembled a flower with the way the steel exterior petaled off into six directions in a semi-symmetrical pattern.

There was a black lump in Harvard's peripheral vision. He turned his head to find that a helmet was lying in the dirt about 15 meters from the carcass of the vehicle. He crept ever so carefully to investigate the helmet when he stopped due to a sound he heard coming from the wreck.

When he turned around facing the vehicle, he found a young man with a smoldering uniform and a face dripping red molten flesh. The man was missing an eye, replaced by shards of broken glass and debris. Blisters dotted his lips, but his entire face was red with exposed muscle and viscera.

The man reached for his handgun in his vest pouch, and put it to his head. Before Harvard could even manage to try to stop him, his head exploded into crimson and brain matter, coating the butchered door in a layer of gore.

The shot echoed throughout the desert, pinging between the mountains on each side so that it was heard over and over again, forcing Harvard to relive what he had just seen in front of him with each reverberation.

He felt his boots carrying himself forward, not his legs. His boots lifted themselves off the ground, pushing Harvard forward, step by step. His blouse sleeves reaching downward to the grotesque scene that lay before him, his gloves moving through the man's collar to inspect his tags:

Taniguchi

Naoto D.

620-50-3286

O Pos

Christian

Harvard let a single tear run down his cheek, "I'm sorry."

CHAPTER 10 - THE LITTLE TOWN IN THE VALLEY

There was a thump that shook Harvard out of his trance, causing him to quickly spin around and point his weapon at the contact. "Harvard?" A voice pierced the smoke, although he couldn't quite make out the speaker. He heard the faint sound of boots on a gravely road, which somehow calmed him a bit. Carl's face emerged from the smoke, in the Texan's hands was his M14. When his mind registered that he was no longer in danger, he lowered his handgun to his side and returned it to it's holster.

Carl slowly walked forward until he was one pace from his friend, who simply stared blankly into the distance. Carl glanced behind him, then back to his squad leader. He gave Harvard a silent nod before handing him his rifle.

"Harvard!" Paul called from the MRAP, prompting both Carl and Harvard to make their way to the passenger door and address the Lieutenant. "Stern has convinced Levi to continue the assault, despite the casualties."

"Is that man nuts? Two vicks are completely fucked, which takes out two fire teams easy!" Abram sounded absolutely furious, but sighed and began climbing out of the car. "Lace your face stompers, boys. Looks like we're marching."

"Uh, Harv, status on Vick 1?" Paul asked.

"Yeah…" His eyes fell upon the gravel road, "They're gone."

"Oh." His expression was blank, "I'll radio that in. Unfortunate." There were a few moments of silence that followed, "You should get going."

Harvard didn't say a word and simply joined the rest of his squad who had moved into a loose column formation. "Forward!" Abram began his order but Paul stepped out of the vehicle to stop him. He whispered something into his ear, causing the Master Sergeant to groan in displeasure. "Are you serious?" He asked, prompting Paul to say something inaudible. "Fuck my pee-hole with a shotgun." He sighed. "Alright, we'll get it done." Paul preformed an about face, and marched back to the relative safety of the crashed MRAP. There was a slight pause before the deafening sound of Abram's voice snapped everyone back into an odd sense of reality. "March!"

The only sound heard was the crunching of dirt underneath boots and the occasional breeze of warm air whistling past the soldier's ears. It was just the desert, the infantrymen, and the silence, until the silence was broken. "Are we there yet?" Carl asked, his voice just barely louder than the sound of the men's footfalls.

"Shut the fuck up, Carl." Abram growled.

Harvard turned his head to the side, allowing his eyes to meet Carl's, who replied with nothing, and just looked down at his shoes, watching them fall upon the sand. He seemed transfixed on them, almost as if the secrets of reality were written in the blood and dirt stains covering the tan canvas. Perhaps Carl should be mesmerized; today he was a real soldier.

But then again, as Harvard pondered, Carl seemed to look down at his boots not with the stare of a fresh out of basic soldier. That focus was the coveted thousand yard stare that only those who have seen the darkest parts of the human race obtain after prolonged exposure to the tendrils of hate. It didn't even seem forced to Harvard, as he had seen the same stare on so many of the people in Birkinistan. Carl's thousand yard stare was genuine.

"Carl." He whispered. The Texan did nothing, he continued watching his feet hit the dirt with the rhythmic and cathartic crunching of the course earth. "Carl." Harvard whispered, louder this time. Still, he did nothing to acknowledge Harvard's attempts to signal him. Harvard simply sighed and moved his attention to the burning sensation on his back, courtesy of that ever present ball of fire in the sky.

The men marched ever further into the desert, until they reached the base of a steep hill where Abram ordered the men to halt. He turned himself to face them and announced, "Congratu-fuckin'-lations. You assholes just entered a combat zone. Now raise your hand if you've ever been in a combat zone before." Fern raised his hand, prompting Harvard to raise an eyebrow at him.

"It's a long story, brohamski." Fern smirked. Abram rolled his eyes and addressed Carl and Harvard.

"This is mainly for you two then. Out here you got two goals: don't get killed, and more importantly, don't get me killed. Any questions?" Abram asked. Carl in his naivety, raised his hand making Harvard cringe.

Before the squad leader could do anything to stop the private, he asked, "Abram, what are we supposed to be doing out here?" His voice held a childlike innocence unparalleled by any living man in this desert.

"Oh shit. I didn't tell you?" A shiver ran down Harvard's spine, "We're clearing houses."

"Oh no… you can't be serious…" Harvard's voice trailed off, nearly trembling in his boots.

"I wish I was joking. I've been there. I've done it. It's not a good time, to say the least." Abram looked around a bit, "Either way, it'll be good to cure some of that so called 'PTSD' you got. More than likely you'll get to turn some goat-groapers into piles of red squishy goo."

Harvard felt his stomach flip upside-down in his torso, the contents sloshing around as though it were a washing machine from hell on the "insanity" setting. He found his knees growing weaker. Everyone knew what happened to the unfortunate souls who were sent to clear houses. They were the ones who slept in the wooden boxes on the side of the runway.

"Oh yeah one more thing." Abram broke Harvard's trance, "We're looking for chemical weapons. Apparently they have a large stockpile of some nasty shit here. Enough to cause another incident like in the Southern Province. Basically if it moves, and it ain't in green, put a hole in it."

"Wait." Fern raised his hand, "What about civilians?"

"Unless you can for sure ID them as unarmed, don't hesitate to take them out." Abram checked the surrounding hilltops once more, "Any further questions?" Nobody raised their hands.

Without even having to say a word, the men started marching up the hill. It didn't feel like Harvard consciously made the decision to advance to the top of the hill, but instead some unseen force moved his boots forward, and thus the rest of his body followed.

As the men neared the peak, they started to hear the muffled pops and bangs of a firefight perhaps miles away, however everyone was well aware that this exchange of gunfire was anywhere but in the distance. It was just in the flat land that inevitably was beyond the peak of this hill. Instantly, Harvard's mind returned to the deafening explosion of crimson and brain matter that he willed into existence in Gamarra. Of course that's where it went, there wasn't anywhere else it could go.

Eventually they crested the peak to over a small town. The hill provided a great vantage point. From there, almost every entrance to the town was visible, and all of them were blocked off by friendly armor. The town was completely surrounded by American forces, rendering any chance for the enemy to escape impossible. They could only hide while friendly forces methodically searched every nook and cranny of that town.

Of course, the town wasn't silent. From their perch above, Harvard watched as the streets flooded with black smoke, and tracer rounds flew from the hillsides surrounding the town, as well as from out of the town itself. The Birkinistanis were putting up as great of a fight to retain this position as they could with the limited materiel they had. The American blockade that was put in place prevented any chance for Saifullah's forces to resupply his men.

"How many of them are in there, you reckon?" Fern asked.

"Dumbasses in command said there's at least 30 squads in there." Abram paused, "But, we have no idea how many of them we've already shot."

"An estimate?" Harvard asked.

"Judging by the knocked out BTR sitting in the road over there," he pointed to a pillar of smoke that sat between two houses on either side of the street, "We've got a pretty good number of them down."

"Ah yeah, that makes sense." Carl added, even though Harvard was about ninety percent certain he didn't hear the first parts of the conversation. "So we're all going to die here?" His voice was as casual as it would be if he was talking about the weather. He was far too calm to be aware that he was inches from death.

Harvard was taken aback by this. An apathetic Carl was a terrifying prospect, as it was him that normally was the one who seemed so happy about things. He looked back to his friend, watching him watch nothingness.

Then he realized something dreadful: he too had the thousand yard stare. He watched Carl a thousand yards from him, and yet still he stood an arm's length away. His head turned to the town in the valley, a stone's throw from his position and yet it too was a thousand yards from him. Harvard was exactly one thousand yards from his friends, the town, Birkinistan, the world, the universe.

"Harvard!" Abram's voice echoed through the abyss that separated him from the universe, and smacked him so hard he was propelled exactly one thousand yards forward until his mind returned to its rightful place in his skull.

"Yes sir—I mean sergeant!" Harvard's heart started racing in his chest, thumping faster and harder than the machine-guns in the town below.

"We're moving." he grunted. Harvard gave a silent nod before the men preceded down the slope. He felt completely uneasy, the slope was so open, there was no cover anywhere. If they were spotted, they would have to make a mad sprint down as fast as their boots could carry them or they'd all be killed. It was such a foolish plan that could be the last mistake they'd ever make.

Ranger didn't seem to worry about the war at all. He wagged his tail, tongue flopping out of his maw as he trotted next to Harvard down the hill. The gunfire in the distance was of no concern to him. As long as nothing was an immediate danger, he was content with running around with his friends. It was all just a fun game to him.

But then he stopped. The men didn't notice and continued their march down he slope. Ranger sniffed the air, then bared his teeth. Still, the men didn't notice the gap that was between them and the yellow dog. A single muted bark escaped his mouth, making all of the men halt at the same time.

That was the only cue they would need. Weapons ready, the men scanned the area with precision and absolute attentiveness. Harvard addressed Ranger, checking to see what direction the dog was pointed. Though Ranger's purpose in the field was to sniff bombs, the dog still knew the enemy almost as if he reached into the confines of Harvard's mind to know who was trying to kill his master. "Contact right side." Harvard reported as he surveyed the hillside. Through a shrubbery almost two hundred yards away, Harvard noticed the unmistakable rise and fall of a man's chest. The men quickly snapped to survey the direction Harvard was looking, and Ranger was pointing.

"That's one of them." Abram announced in a hushed tone, though his men could clearly hear what he was saying.

"Let's fuck him up." Fern smirked.

"Maybe he's just a civilian hiding." Harvard suggested, still aligning his scope reticle on the shrub.

"Civilians don't carry AK's. Fire on my go." Abram's words stung, leaving a sour taste in Harvard's mouth. Ranger positioned himself so that he was directly in front of Harvard, his flank exposed to the direction of the enemy.

"Kill him." Carl muttered, just audible enough for Harvard to hear. Then Harvard's hearing cut out from the monstrous sound of a 5.56 NATO cartridge's primer being struck by the firing pin of an M16A2 combat rifle.

Training kicked in and before the sound could clear from Harvard's mind, he was on the floor as flat as he could possibly be. His finger had disengaged the safety of the rifle and was pointed at the enemy. Without hesitating, or without consciously acting on the decision, he squeezed the trigger with a thunderous roar that even forced the dirt to fly into the air. He had no idea if he hit the man, or if he just shot another civilian, or if he missed completely.

Soon the nook between the slope and the town that Harvard and his friends had found themselves in lit up with the sound of rifle fire. It was too much, too loud, too surreal for Harvard to even process what was happening until it all stopped. The conflict in the town hadn't, but the symphony of destruction within that tiny stretch of land had ceased without anyone saying a word.

Harvard waited, cheek pressed to his rifle, finger still on the trigger, safety still disengaged. He waited for two words that would allow him to get back on his feet and continue his march into the hell that was the town. Those words never came.

Instead what Harvard heard was the cracking of a bullet passing over his head, followed by several more, followed by cracks and green tracers flying with the intention to put a hole in him so that he could no longer stand, walk, fight, or even live. He felt bile rise in his throat, but he pushed it down and instead of throwing up, he threw hot lead. He used the tracers as a line to follow to the enemy's positions, and mashed the trigger over and over again to maximize his chances of hitting an enemy.

He didn't know how long it took, but the order to move was shouted through the chaos, forced from Abram's mouth. Harvard's gloves forced his rifle to act as an aid to stand himself up, but a green tracer instantly forced him back to the ground out of pure terror. The bullet nicked the strap of his vest on his right shoulder, leaving a bit of torn fabric on his shoulder.

He had to move, but he wasn't sure how. If he stood up, he lost the tiny amount of cover he had and would be killed, but if he stayed the enemy would move and he would be killed. "Fuck!" He exclaimed before a stupid idea popped into his head: he could roll down the slope.

Another "Fuck!" escaped his lips before he came to the realization that if he would die if he didn't move, and at least with this stupid idea he had the chance to survive. He put his rifle back on safe, and then used it to push himself down the slope with as much force as he could muster.

Then the world was on spin cycle as Harvard hit every rock and bump he possibly could've on his descent down into the town, gathering momentum and velocity with each revolution until he crashed right into the side of a house. He felt his equipment slam into the white wall of the house, and then into his squishy flesh by consequence.

Without skipping a beat, Harvard was back on his feet, rifle at the ready. The symphony came to an abrupt, yet ominous standstill. The green beams of light zipping through the nook between the houses and the hillside halted as though a thousand sergeants called the command to cease fire all at once.

A hand grabbed Harvard's shoulder, and in an act of survival instinct he spun around ready to fire at whoever was behind him. But he didn't. Instead of the eyes of the enemy, his eyes met the eyes of his friend. A friendly, familiar face staring at him, but for the life of him Harvard couldn't remember the name. His eyes glanced to the right of the man's chest to read "Fern" in plain black text on the Army Universal Camouflage Pattern. This man was his friend, and was not going to hurt him.

Behind Fern were the others, all three of them survived and were unharmed, relatively speaking. Abram's face was covered in dirt, and Carl had a scratch across his forehead from the brambles on the hillside.

The world slowed to half step, and Harvard got to bear witness to every muscle in Abram's face twist and contort to form a circle with his lips. Then the world sped to normal pace instantaneously as though the command Abram called was "Forward, march!" but instead it was much more terrifying: "Move!"

Then the wall started crumbling around them as fresh holes were punched into it by bits of lead slamming into it at velocities faster than the words could escape Harvard's mouth. "Fuck! Fuck! Fuck! Shit! Fuck! Fuck!"

The next time Harvard's mind began consciously realizing the world was happening, he was in a house with his friends around him. Dusty stone floors were covered in crimson and bullet casings. He was covered in blood, but wasn't in any amount of pain that would suggest he was injured. He looked around and found that within the chest of a Birkinistani soldier was an M9 bayonet, and Harvard's was missing from his pouch. A few fleeting flashbacks popped into his head—he dropped his rifle and rammed the bayonet into this enemy soldier's chest with as much strength as he could muster.

He looked at his hands to see his gloves were stained red, his uniform was wet with the clotting gore of his adversary. He looked around the room looking for his dog. There was nothing he wanted more than to simply lay down and cry with that yellow ball of fur and love. He couldn't. His dog was in the corner of the room, sitting attentively with a fresh coating of blood on his muzzle. "What happened to him?" He asked to anyone, anyone who would listen to him. It didn't matter.

"He's fine, he took a bit of a spill coming down the slope, but he's okay. The blood's not his, it's this guy's." Abram pushed the dead man's torso with his boot. Harvard's eyes scanned the corpse and found that the man's left leg had been completely shredded by what appeared to be a set of teeth. "Heh. He got you good in the head too."

"How…" Harvard trailed off. He once again fell bile rise to his throat, this time he couldn't force it down and it all came out of his mouth, mixing with the crimson stained dirt. After he recovered, he ejected the magazine from his rifle to find that it was empty, meaning he had one single round in his chamber. With an uncontrollably shaking hand, he dropped the magazine on the floor and he retrieved a new one from his vest, and through muscle memory placed it in the magazine well of his rifle.

His boots carried him forward so that he could remove the knife implanted into the man's chest. With a forceful tug, he removed his knife from the man's chest, causing more of that sticky, red liquid to spray out. He sighed, wiping the knife on his trouser leg until the matte black metal was clean. He returned the knife to its holster on his belt, and made his way over to Ranger.

As Harvard's back pressed against the wall of the house, he couldn't help but try to replay the events that took place before now. He tried his very best to attempt to piece together all the bits of fragmented memories that had been struck out of his mind, perhaps for the better.

He felt Ranger's head on his leg, and with a glance down at the dog, found a streak of fresh blood along his back. His yellow fur was in clumps, glued together by the vital fluid and dirt. If Ranger was injured in any way, he couldn't tell at all; the dog seemed perfectly fine to him, say for being a bit dirty.

Harvard began staring off into the distance, while the rest of the men silently got their bearings as well. The rest of the world, was anything but silent. Outside the white wash walls of the house still played the orchestra of war, trumpets of machine guns, violins of violence, no conductor to be seen. War stops for no man.

The vest on Harvard's shoulders seemed to be heavier than when he first put it on this morning, even his uniform that he wore every single day while he was deployed seemed even heavier. The entire world seemed heavier and one thousand yards away. He opened his lips ever so slightly to speak, but unsure of what to say. But he spoke regardless, "What now?" It was all he could manage to ask, the war unfolding in front of him was too great to process. It was something he was never even meant to understand. Something nobody was meant to understand.

Abram studied the dead man on the floor, making mental notes of every inch of his solid tan colored fatigues. He then focused his attention on Harvard, who sat on the floor with the dog's head resting on his shin. "Well, we can't go outside because we'd be in view of the Haji snipers, but they can't come in here because the camel-fuckers will be in view of our snipers. So we're stuck in this shit hole until the cavalry arrives." Abram spat on the corpse.

"When's that?" Fern asked, an odd sense of urgency in his voice.

"20:00 hours. Cav scouts should be here. Your girlfriend too, Harvard." Abram teased.

"She's not my girlfriend." Harvard wasn't paying attention to Abram too much, he was a thousand yards away.

"Sarge, that's like four hours from now." Carl groaned.

"Then ladies, you better get your asses comfortable. We'll be shitting in here until Harvard's bitch gets her fine ass in gear." Abram prodded at Harvard further, but he didn't respond. Harvard was still listening to the war beyond the thin walls of the house. This was his life now.

CHAPTER 11 - THE CORPSMAN

It was 20:28 when the cavalry arrived to relieve Harvard and the others from their trapped position in the house. The engines of the vehicles was audible through the walls of the house, through the machine guns and fighting that hadn't slowed in the slightest. With the roaring of the armored beasts outside the house, Harvard knew it was time to move. The blood had long since dried on his uniform, painting the dull green colors a new sickly shade of red.

He stood up, collecting his rifle and other supplies, although he left the bag that once housed his beef ravioli MRE on the floor. It served it's purpose, and now was nothing more than a bag full of garbage.

The familiar sound of boots thunking on stone floors filled Harvard's ears, never mind that of the war outside. "Are we ready to move?" He asked with a yawn. Harvard had begun to feel the effects of exhaustion take a toll on his mind, however small that toll may be. He knew it was only a matter of time before he would be bested by his exhaustion, but have to push through it regardless.

Abram gathered his belongings from the floor, then kicked Fern in the boot, who was fast asleep and using an empty plastic water bottle as a pillow. As his head rose, the bottle crunched and whined as it returned to its desired form. "What? We moving?" He asked.

Harvard shifted his attention to Carl, who was sitting in the corner of his house, scribbling away in his black journal with a ball point pen. He almost didn't want to disturb him, he looked so entranced in his work, but before he could do anything, Abram's voice shook the planks of wood that sat beneath them.

"Alright, shit stains! On your feet! We're going Haji hunting!" With a sigh, Carl wrote his last thoughts down onto the paper, then returned his journal to his vest pocket. His eyes met Harvard's, and although they exchanged no words with each other. Harvard knew exactly what Carl was thinking: he wanted to go home.

With that, the men all crept out of the house to find that the street they were on had been blocked off by a line of vehicles only about one hundred yards from their position. Immediately they were spotted and identified as friendly by the cavalry.

This was the first time Harvard had actually been able to take a good look at the town around him, which was to say that it was very dilapidated. Many of the typical Birkinistani homes had been perforated by bullets, pillars of black smoke could be seen rising throughout the town.

"Gentlemen! I'm so glad to see you're all alright." Harvard turned his head away from the smoke pillars to find First Lieutenant Paul standing across from them with two other soldiers from Third Squad standing to his right and left.

"Yeah, we're all good here, Paul. Do we continue as planned?" Abram asked. He looked around the street to find that almost all of the houses around still had their doors closed and didn't have any signs that they were searched at all.

"Did you guys… even search the homes?" He seemed to be slightly agitated that no progress had been made.

"No, sir. We got pinned down by enemy snipers on the ridge. Now that the cavalry is here, we can get to work." Carl smiled, however his explanation did nothing to thwart Paul's palm smacking his face with a loud clap.

"God damn it…" He growled, "The houses were supposed to be cleared so that some slushy slinger doesn't sling an RPG into the cavalry!"

An audible "fuck" escaped Harvard's mouth. "Well what do we do?" He asked, shifting uncomfortably in his boots.

"Well, I guess there's only one thing you can do. You have to clear the houses. Go get it done, and hopefully everyone of you will still have all their limbs attached and blood inside their body. By the way, Harvard, is that your blood?" The lieutenant pointed at Harvard's blood soaked trousers. The private shook his head in response. "Good, I was gonna say. I mean that's a lot of blood."

The men exchanged goodbyes, then they began moving towards the houses that were parallel to the road the cavalry would be driven along. Harvard counted at least sixteen houses he and the others would have to clear before the convoy could push any further up into the town.

The men reached the door of the first house they would have to search, a maroon wooden door stood between them an uncertain death. There could've been any number of things behind that door — a man with a rifle, a deranged civilian with a machete, perhaps even a rabid dog — but all those possibilities collapsed in on themselves the moment Abram kicked in the door. Nothing was there.

Even still, the house was two floors, and they could only see into the living room of that first floor. The men quickly moved in, checking the corners of the room, under furniture, every hiding spot in the room, then moved on to the makeshift kitchen where they checked every hiding place there too. That was the first floor, just a living room that appeared to have been converted into some sort of bedroom for guests that perhaps weren't meant to be there in the first place, and a pathetic excuse for a kitchen.

Fern took point as he and Harvard moved up the stairs to investigate the second floor which was just a bedroom and a small washroom. They checked every possible hiding place in the upper floor of the house, finding that it was completely vacant. It appeared that nobody had been there for quite some time.

Harvard poked his head down the stairs and sounded off, "Clear!" Both he and Fern returned downstairs to the rest of the men, and they all exited the house together as one single unit. Before the men could move on to the next house, Abram removed a small bottle of orange spray paint and painted a large "C" on the wall facing the street.

Then they repeated the process with the second house, finding that it too was clear, and the third, and the fourth, and so on. Each house they breached and cleared was completely empty. By this point, the men seemed to be more at ease with the situation, as it appeared the worst of the assault on this town was over.

By the sixth house, Carl was given the opportunity to breach the door. He politely knocked on it and with a shrill voice exclaimed, "Knock knock! Girl Scout Cookies!" He then kicked the door with all his might, completely breaking the door off it's hinges. To the men's surprise, this house wasn't empty. Staring Harvard directly in the eye was a small child in a red and white patterned shirt and black pants.

"On your knees!" Abram shouted at the top of his lungs, prompting the little boy to put his hands up in surrender. Harvard immediately recognized the boy's gaze as his own — the thousand yard stare. This boy had seen the horrors of war firsthand.

Sickened by this, Harvard forced Abram's muzzle up towards the ceiling to address the boy. He figured the poor child didn't speak english, which was alright. It was perhaps better that way. "He's just a fucking kid! Leave him alone!" Harvard ordered his superior. Abram sighed, but returned to his normal state of noncommissioned agitation. Harvard carried himself to the boy, then gestured for the rest of the men to search the house for hostiles or other civilians. "Family?" Harvard asked, seeing if the boy could understand him at all.

The boy stared up at the strange soldier in front of him, and with tears forming in his eyes said, "No ingish." Harvard nodded in understanding, and reached down to grab his canteen from his belt. He held it out to the boy as an offering of friendship.

The boy in the red shirt fixed his gaze on the canteen Harvard held out, and with a shaking hand clasped onto it. He unscrewed the cap and took a large gulp from the canteen, then tried to return it to Harvard. He refused it, holding up his hand as if to say "keep it". He then reached into his vest pouch to remove a protein bar that was still wrapped and untouched, and held it out to the boy.

Abram's voice boomed throughout the house as he yelled, "Clear!" Harvard breathed a sigh of relief. The boy sitting in front of him cocked his head slightly as though he didn't understand what the object Harvard was holding was, prompting him to unwrap the bar and show the boy that it was in fact food. Upon this realization, the boy quickly grabbed the bar from Harvard and took a large bite out of it.

The boy's sad brown eyes met Harvard's once more, and a faint "*Shukraan*," escaped the boy's mouth. He understood the arabic word for "thank you", or at least that's what he figured the boy said.

He returned with his own, "*Afwan*," the arabic word for "you're welcome." Those were the only two things Harvard understood in the boy's native language, but they were the only two things he needed to understand.

Abram's hand met Harvard's shoulder, "We have to move. More houses." He looked up to the sergeant and nodded, but he didn't want to leave the boy here alone any longer. In this boy he saw the boy in the black shirt, and the atrocity he committed upon him. He wasn't going to let another child die.

"Can we bring him to the cavalry?" He asked. Abram looked down at the child, not feeling the same connection that Harvard did to him.

"I suppose we can push the little fucker towards them. Someone will take care of him, bring him to Gamarra or something… probably." That was enough for him. He gently grabbed hold of the boy's free hand.

He gazed back into the boy's eyes and whispered, "It's going to be okay. We're going to help you. We're going to bring you to safety." Harvard knew the boy didn't understand the words he said, but the boy understood his voice. With a nod, he collected himself, and the two left the house.

"Harvard! We're going to clear seven! Double time back!" Abram called out to Harvard as he, Ranger, and the little boy made their way to the convoy.

"Yes, sergeant!" Harvard replied, then the three continued their walk to the cavalry sitting idly in the street. Harvard didn't let go of the boy's hand, not so much for the child's sake, but more for his own. He looked down at the boy, taking his eyes off the surrounding area for just a moment to talk to boy. "Name?" He asked, unsure if the boy understood what he was asking.

Unfortunately for him, the boy either didn't hear him, or didn't understand what he asked. Harvard shrugged this off, and let his mind wander some more. He wondered what would happen to this poor child who was born in a war zone, and perhaps spent the seven years of his life here. He wasn't even sure he was seven years old, but the child looked to be around that age. He was terrified that the boy would be trapped here without a family and would be rejected by the American forces and would return back to this hell. Harvard wanted to keep this child as his own, raise him to be right, but he knew he couldn't. All he could realistically do for this child was bring him to the cavalry. Then he would no longer be his responsibility, and the child would more than likely be sent to a refugee camp.

Harvard returned to the cavalry with the boy's hand still in his, and made his way to the first soldiers he could find: a female sergeant and an african-american corporal. "Take care of this one, he's been through a lot." Harvard ordered them.

"Understood. Does he have a name?" The sergeant asked.

"I don't know. Do we have an interpreter?"

"Yeah, I speak arabic." The corporal replied.

"Good. I don't want any more harm to come to this poor guy." Harvard looked down to his little friend, who looked back up at him. "It's okay now." Harvard whispered, "You're safe." Almost immediately, tears welled up at the bottom of the boy's eyes, and he hugged Harvard as tightly as he possibly could, causing tears to form in Harvard's eyes.

"*Shukraan*," the boy whispered one final time.

"*Afwan,*" Harvard whispered back. The corporal put his hand on the boy's back, and escorted him to the rear of the cavalry where he would be safest with the sergeant as their escort. Harvard knew this would be the last time he'd ever see that child, which forced one single tear to slide down his dirty and blood stained cheek, leaving one single streak of pink flesh exposed.

Harvard's gloved hand met Ranger's head to scratch behind his ear, then the two marched back towards the houses that the rest of his companions would be. The sound of conflict in the air blocked out the familiar sound of boots on pavement, filling him with a sense of unease. In the street, he found the rotting corpse of a stray dog being picked apart by birds. He quickly reached down to pet Ranger, as in that corpse he saw his childhood dog, Ruger. "Not you, boy." He whispered to his yellow friend walking next to him.

He reached the house Abram said he was going to clear, and found a large orange "C" painted on the wall next to the now broken door. Inside he saw the rotting corpse of a woman in traditional black clothing, covering her from head to toe, say for the fact that her head was missing. She looked like she had been dead for quite some time, there was no way anyone of Harvard's squad mates had done that to her. She obviously wasn't beheaded, as it appeared that someone had taken a shotgun and blew her head off. He kept moving.

He reached the house that his friends obviously had broken into, and sounded off, "Friendly moving in!" So the men knew not to shoot him while he entered the building. With a careful step, he moved in through the large hole made in the door by what appeared to be a lot of different people kicking the door at once. Perhaps Abram, Fern, and Carl all kicked the door at the same time as they were starting to get exhausted from continuous door kicking.

Carl's voice echoed throughout the house, "Clear!" Prompting Harvard to feel more at ease in that one building. Abram appeared from the kitchen, while both Fern and Carl moved down the stairs making as much noise as they possibly could.

"Come on, ladies, we got more houses!" Abram ordered, forcing the sweating, tired, broken, and defeated men to trek forward. They all moved as one synchronized unit out of the house and towards the next, where they simply tried to open the door normally, finding that it was in fact unlocked. They repeated the process of clearing each room, reporting clear, and painting the "C", before moving on.

On house twelve, Carl decided to kick down the door himself. He knocked on the door politely as he always did, then in his best impression of a priest asked, "Excuse me, do you have a moment to talk about freedom?"

"Shut the fuck up, Carl." Abram muttered, then Carl kicked the door with all his might, blowing it right off it's hinges. There was a loud bang, followed by Abram firing into the dark house, and a yelp from Ranger. Harvard spun around to face his dog to find that he was on the floor and bleeding heavily.

"No." Harvard muttered, then disregarded the men firing into the house and rushed as fast as he could to his dog who was now a casualty. "No! Fuck! No!" Ranger was bleeding profusely from his right hind leg. Harvard picked up his dog and brought him behind cover, where he stayed with him, applying as much pressure to the wound as he could. "Hang in there, boy! We're going to get you out of here!" Harvard shouted, tears in his eyes.

He heard footsteps from behind him, so with one hand he held Ranger's wound, and the other he drew his handgun and pointed it at the direction of the noise. "Harvard!" It was only Carl, prompting him to lower his weapon. "Oh God. Harvard, he's hit."

With a rage that couldn't be subsided, Harvard's eyes shot fire at Carl as he shouted, "I fucking know that! Get me a God damned corpsman, right fucking now!" Without hesitation, Carl sprinted towards the cavalry as fast as his boots could carry him. Harvard continued to apply pressure to his dog's freshly punched hole in his leg, screaming at his dog that he would save him. "You're going to be okay, I promise. I'm going to save you." He was drenched head to toe in blood, sweat, and tears.

It felt like forever, listening to his best friend scream in agony. The deafening sounds of shooting couldn't drown out the horrifying sounds of a dog in extreme pain. Nothing in his entire life could ever prepare him for this, no amount of training ever could. His friends could be dying in that house right behind him, but there was no way he was going to leave Ranger.

"You're going to be okay. I know it hurts, I know, I know. But it looks like the bleeding is going away, at least a little bit." Harvard's voice shook. He wasn't sure if he was crying or not, all he knew was his best friend was dying and he wasn't going to let that happen. There was no way he was going to let his dog die.

Carl returned with three other soldiers, two armed with rifles, the other was carrying a massive backpack full of medical supplies. Harvard kept holding pressure on the dog's leg as the medic knelt down beside him and assessed the damage. The corpsman looked at Harvard's blood soaked uniform and asked, "How much of that is his?"

He checked his uniform as he continued to apply pressure to his dog's wound and replied, "I have no fucking clue!" He shouted, "Just fix my fucking dog!" The corpsman was unfazed by the yelling.

"Alright, lift your hands, let's see what I'm working with." The corpsman's orders quickly made Harvard pick his hands up off Ranger's wound. His gloves were completely trashed, there was no salvaging them, so he removed them and tossed them aside. The corpsman smiled as he tore open a package of QuikClot to begin packing the wound, "Well, we got some good news. The bullet didn't hit any veins or arteries, it didn't touch the bone, and it went clean through. You are super lucky, if it was a millimeter higher, your dog would be bleeding to death. I can save him, and we'll bring him back to Ulysses where we can get him on his feet in as little as twelve weeks."

Harvard laughed a little, but still couldn't help but let a few more tears stream down his face. Carl's hand found his shoulder, "Here that, Reggie? He's going to be okay." He could tell that the Texan was crying a bit too.

Harvard's hand moved behind Ranger's floppy ear and scratched the soft fur. His eyes found his dog's, and he whispered,

"You're going to be okay, boy." Ranger gave a little whimper as though he understood what his friend had just told him.

The corpsman wrapped an elastic bandage around the dog's leg as tightly as he could make it, then injected a painkiller into the tissue in his neck, which worked quickly, putting the dog in a trance like state. "Okay gents, get this dog out of here, move him in with the wounded. I want him on the first helicopter out, understood?"

"Yes, sir!" The two soldiers shouted in unison. It was only then that Harvard noticed the twin black bars on his shoulder signaling that the corpsman was in fact a captain. It didn't matter to him; his dog was going to be alright.

"I love you, Ranger." Harvard whispered as he planted a kiss on the dog's head, which he returned with a weak lick to the cheek, as if he were wiping the tears away. With that, the two soldiers picked Ranger up and quickly rushed him to the cavalry in the distance.

Harvard stood up, eyes still fixed on the pool of blood that stained the floor where his dog once was. He wiped the tears away one last time, replacing the clean streaks on his cheeks with a new coating of smeared crimson. He slowly turned around to face the house, where he found Abram and Fern standing outside. Abram was painting the "C" on the wall, while Fern flipped off the house as though it were a sentient object that could understand what he was saying.

Harvard and Carl walked side by side to return to the men where without so much as a pause, Harvard demanded, "Is the one who shot Ranger dead?" Abram smiled and pointed at the house.

"Not yet." He snickered. Harvard looked inside the broken down door of the house to see a man bleeding from his stomach on the floor, his weapon was too far for him to grab, and he looked too weak to do anything. Abram elbowed Harvard lightly on the shoulder. "He's all yours, private."

With a smile, he crept into the house, where his eyes met those of the dying man on the floor. The man wheezed and gagged as blood sprayed out of his mouth, pooling into puddles on his cheeks as it coagulated. The man had a perfectly punched hole in his abdomen, right beneath the sternum. This was the man who shot Ranger.

Harvard knelt down beside him, watching the excruciating rise and fall of his chest, listening to the labored breathing. This man couldn't be saved, this man simply had to die. He wanted so bad to sit and watch him die. "You know you shot my best friend, right?" He murmured. The man didn't react, simply kept his eyes transfixed on Harvard's as if to say, "Just shoot me."

Something within was telling him to shoot the man on the floor, simply to put this soldier out of his misery, whereas the rage and hatred within him told him to force the man to stand by and suffer. "I'm debating on if I'm going to put a bullet in your head or not." He told him, who still did nothing to react. "It doesn't matter, you're going to die regardless."

Harvard's heart was beating ever so quickly, there was too much adrenaline in his veins from everything that had happened that day. "Unlike my dog. He'll be okay." The man coughed, spraying more blood onto Harvard's uniform. He didn't care. He knew that once he was done here he was going to simply toss this set of ACUs into the garbage and pick up a new set, boots and all.

The man's eyes were an unexpected color. They were an icy blue, unlike the brown that most of the people in this part of the world had. Harvard found them disgusting. This man's blood soaked face made him want to puke. Every tiny detail about this man was repulsive. He wasn't even certain that this creature dying in front of him was a human being.

"I hate you." Harvard hissed. The man either didn't understand or didn't care what he was saying, as he simply stayed transfixed on Harvard's eyes. Never once did the man make any attempt to grab Harvard's handgun, which was only a few inches from the man's blood stained hands. "I never thought I could hate anyone this much, but you proved me wrong." Harvard's hands formed fists, forcing the wet clotted blood to squelch, further adding to his disgust.

He almost wanted to pound the man's head into a gooey mess of brain matter, flesh, blood and bone fragments, but Harvard's primal desire to watch as the man suffered overcame him. He simply stared into the icy blue eyes of the enemy, watching the man choke on his own blood and spit with a smirk of triumph plastered on his face. "I'm enjoying this." He chuckled, still knowing that the man didn't understand what he was saying. He didn't care. He was happily watching every moment of this go on. "I wish I had a bucket of popcorn right now."

As those words left his mouth, Harvard realized what he was doing. He realized that this monster dying before him wasn't a monster at all: he was a human. This man was dying, and Harvard no longer felt disgusted about having to look at the horrible creature that shot his dog, but rather he was disgusted by himself. His smirk faded at the cognizance of what war had turned him into. Harvard was as much of a monster as the man on the floor was.

The dying man let out another cough, followed by a labored wheeze, his eyes still transfixed on Harvard's. "*Sa—*" The man said weakly, blood dripping out of his mouth as the man attempted to speak. Harvard squinted, his eyebrows furrowed, slightly agitated that the man suddenly now had something to say to him, but still curious as to what the man even could possibly say.

Then Harvard's desires for revenge bubbled up to the surface once more, remembering what this man did to his best friend. Nothing he could say or do could possibly make him think differently about this man. The screams of his best friend echoed in his mind as the wheezes of the dying man echoed in the dark house. Nothing could drive those screams of agony out of Harvard's mind for as long as he'd live.

The man opened his mouth once more, and with a labored inhale of precious air, attempted to speak once more. His voice was like sand paper on a chalk board, "*Sami—*" the man couldn't finish his sentence as he choked on his blood, forcing a blood clot to escape his throat and fall upon the man's chest.

The man inhaled once more, "*Samihni.*" He knew the end was near for this pathetic excuse for a human being, his words meaning nothing. Harvard figured the man simply swore at him, or was requesting for him to shoot him; something he wouldn't do. This was too perfect.

"Yeah? Fuck you too." He replied, eyes never leaving the man's face. The man coughed and gagged on another blood clot, and he went silent once more. The man simply stared deep into Harvard's eyes, as Harvard stared back into the icy blue irises of the enemy.

But the man opened his mouth once more to speak, "*Samih —*" Harvard almost went deaf. He jumped and blinked to find that the man's head had all but exploded on one side, as there was a small hole in the left side of his head, and a grapefruit size hole in the right. Harvard looked around the room to find that Carl was standing over him with an M9 handgun in his right hand.

He holstered the weapon, and reached downward to help Harvard to his feet. Their eyes met. "You know what he said, right?" Carl asked.

Harvard simply shook his head. "I assumed he was just cursing at me." He replied. Carl sighed and reached down to pick up Harvard's M14 from the floor.

"No, he wasn't swearing." Carl's held out Harvard's rifle for him.

"Really? What'd he say?" Harvard asked as he took back his rifle.

"I'm sorry."

CHAPTER 12 - STERN

American forces had successfully occupied the town, forcing the Birkinistanis out in just under fifteen hours. They were able to uncover enough sarin gas to kill everyone in a town of the same size as this one. There were only thirty-six injuries on the American front, whereas a total of one-hundred-forty-one Birkinistani combatants were either injured or killed. Civilian casualties were in the high fifties, with the majority of them being killed in action, and the majority of the injuries being critical. Many of them wouldn't be able to be saved.

Harvard awoke in a cot and sleeping bag at around 05:45, well before the sun had peeked its head out from behind the mountains surrounding the town. He hadn't slept well at all during the night, the faces of war haunted his dreams. He had contributed to three of the one-hundred-forty-one casualties on the opposing side of the conflict, which was a whole two percent. His best friend consisted of two percent of the American casualties as well. Though Harvard wasn't sure, he thought that most of the nightmares he had were about watching Ranger die in front of him.

Deciding that it was a good of a time as any to be awake, he climbed out of his cot and slipped his boots on, which were still covered in blood and dirt. His uniform was also still stained, along with his skin. These stains would forever remind him of what he did in this little town in the valley. With a sigh, Harvard finished lacing his boots and began walking hazily towards the sound of voices to perhaps obtain a cup of hot coffee and a breakfast MRE.

To his dismay, the voices he found were that of First Lieutenant Paul, and Second Lieutenant Stern. He growled as he saluted the two men, which Paul returned, but Stern did not. "You're in a combat zone," He scoffed, "You don't salute here."

"Good morning to you too, asshole." Harvard began walking past the two officers, but Paul put his hand on his shoulder.

"You'll be happy to hear that Ranger got the attention he needed and is currently in recovery. He'll be ready to return to his duties in about four months time, sixteen weeks." He said with a warm smile. "He's going to be just fine. I'm sorry you had to see all of that."

Harvard smiled and patted Paul on the shoulder, "He would've stood by for me if I was the one hit." Paul nodded an understandingly. Harvard then refocused his attention to Stern, his hands forming fists. "You though. You're the reason he got flown out in a helicopter in the first place."

Stern furrowed his eyebrows and glared at Harvard. "I don't know the slightest thing you're talking about. All I did was convince our CO that action needed to be taken here." Stern grit his teeth as the words escaped his mouth, "Think about this, your dog made a sacrifice that greatly contributed to a huge American victory! It greatly raised the morale of our men and we stopped a potential serious attack. Besides, your mutt is fine."

It required all of Harvard's strength not to punch Stern in the throat at that moment. "He's lucky to be alive." He too grit his teeth as the words left his lips. Stern smiled as the agitated Harvard glared at Stern.

Stern let out a sigh and with a voice as cold as ice told him, "You're lucky to be alive too." The words echoed in the early morning air, resonating off the mountains only to force themselves back into Harvard's ears.

The fire that had been burning inside of him for such a long time, since the first time Harvard's eyes met Stern's, had reached it's highest point. All the kindling, all the fuel that had been dumped into it had combusted at the same point. Harvard lunged forward in an attempt to tackle the Lieutenant and beat his face into the dirt until his head resembled the deceased woman from the day before.

He wasn't able to so much as touch Stern. Paul grabbed onto him before he did anything he would later regret. He looked Harvard directly in the eye, seeing the fire burning within them, and smacked him across the face. "Get ahold of yourself, soldier!" He shouted, snapping Harvard back to reality. The fire within him returned to the smoldering embers that it once was, not extinguished, simply reduced.

Harvard's gaze returned to the Second Lieutenant, and he repeated the same words he said to him, "You're lucky to be alive too." Harvard pushed Paul's arms off of him before walking away to a destination that he wasn't quite sure of yet. He simply didn't want to look at Second Lieutenant Stern any longer.

Eventually, he found a couple men with MRE coffee powder and a surplus of flameless ration heaters. "Battlefield baristas,"

Harvard chuckled under his breath as he walked up to the soldiers setting up shop.

"Hello, uh, Harvard!" The man running the makeshift cashier box had read Harvard's nametape, "Welcome to The Enlisted Lounge! We got black coffee, and that's literally it. It comes in two types, lukewarm and cold, although sometimes lukewarm ends up being actually hot. Cold is three bucks, warm is five. If you order two though, the third is free." The man smiled.

Harvard examined the operation that these men were putting on and asked, "Does the Army know you're doing this with their MREs?" The man shook his head, causing Harvard to giggle. "And who organized this?"

"The boss? Oh, Murray Fern did." Harvard was legitimately impressed with Fern. Perhaps someone didn't need a college degree to be a successful businessman.

With a smile, he ordered a hot cup of coffee, handing over a ten dollar bill. "Thank you, sir. Your order will be ready in a few moments." Harvard simply giggled once again. Turning around the survey the area, he saw Carl sitting alone with his back propped up against the wall of a house. He was writing in his journal again.

Harvard turned around to address the men who were preparing his coffee. "Hey, gents. Can I get another one? I don't need the third, just two hot coffees."

"Absolutely." The man preparing his coffee had such an oddly cheerful voice, almost making Harvard feel uneasy by the whole thing. Even still, he welcomed the idea of a freshly brewed cup of coffee, especially in such early hours of the morning.

Just as the sun first shot its rays over the hillside, the coffee had finished brewing and Harvard was on his way. With both steaming cups of coffee in both his hands, he sat down next to Carl. "Good morning." He said quietly as he held out a cup for Carl.

Looking up from his journal, Carl's eyes met Harvard's forcing a smile on his face. "Howdy." Carl smiled as he gratefully accepted the cup of coffee that had been offered him. "Sleep alright?" He asked.

"No. You?"

"Not a wink." Carl scribbled his last thoughts down into his journal, then closed it with a thump. The two men clinked their Styrofoam cups together, then as one single unit, took a sip of their coffee.

"That's the harsh reality of the combat zone. You either sleep well or not at all." Harvard told Carl as though he had been doing this for quite some time. Both of the men knew that this was the first time Harvard had been a part of actual combat.

Carl sighed, then took another sip of his coffee. "Why are we doing this to ourselves?" His childlike innocence was so pronounced in his question that it very well could have been uttered by a young boy.

Harvard took a sip of his coffee and looked back at his disgusting uniform, every stain of red a reminder of what happened in this town. He took another sip as though that coffee was bourbon to drink away his pain. "I don't know." Harvard whispered. The men simply watched the sun rise over the hills that just yesterday they had fought on, silently sipping on their coffee. It was beautiful, rays of orange and blue overflowing from the hilltops, washing down into the town ever so slightly.

"I think we're going back to Ulysses today, at least after we clean up." Carl told his friend, although both of the men didn't take their eyes off the sunrise, "At least, that's what I heard Paul say when I first climbed out of my cot. Both he and Stern have been up since oh-three." Still Harvard said nothing, as there was nothing to say. It was too early, they had done too much the night before, and both men were still defeated by the ordeal.

The sun continued its advance off the hilltops into the little town in the valley, until the entire town was bathed in a faint blue-yellow glow. It was a beautiful sight to behold, even in Harvard's almost broken state.

Harvard felt Carl's finger poke his forearm, prompting him to address his friend. "Reggie, can I talk about something personal with you?" He asked, a genuine expression of concern on his face.

"Uh, yeah of course." Harvard replied, sort of unsure of how he was supposed to react. Carl smiled and picked up his journal from the dirt he sat in. He brushed the specks of brown off the black leather, and admired it ever so gently.

Slowly and deliberately, Carl opened the journal and began flipping through the pages until he found the one he was looking for. His eyes met Harvard's once more, "Have I told you about her?" Carl asked.

"Her? Who is her?" Harvard asked.

"Daisy Burke?" Harvard shook his head, "Well, she's someone very important to me. Her family took me in when my folks died in Arlington."

"Wait hold on, your parents were killed *there*?"

"That was so long ago, it's irrelevant." He took a deep breath, "Daisy is the love of my life. I promised her I'd come home once this was all over."

Harvard sighed, "Carl... you knew you couldn't make a promise like that..."

"Yeah. She knew that too." Carl sighed and stared off into the distance, "And that's where you come in." He carefully tore the page out of his notebook, then flipped to the last few pages in the back, and tore another out. Carl began folding the paper as he continued talking, "If I can't keep my promise, I want you to deliver this to her." He kept folding the blank paper, "And tell her the one thing I wish I could every morning." Harvard knew what he was about to say, "I need you to tell her that I love her."

His words hit Harvard like a wall of bricks, as Carl finished folding a makeshift envelope with the page from his journal tucked away inside. He held the envelope out to him to take, but Harvard pushed it away.

"You're not going to need me to. I promise." Harvard told him. He just smiled innocently.

"Now you're making promises you can't keep." With those last words, the sun had fully cast the little town in the valley in its normal morning glow. Harvard knew Carl was right, there was no way he could make a promise like that.

Someone started banging on a trash can and shouting to wake everyone who had somehow been able to fall asleep after the fighting. Just a few more hours until Harvard got to return to Ulysses, take a hot shower, and get himself a new set of ACUs from his CHU. This prospect was more than enough to get Harvard on his feet, coffee still in his hands. He looked down to Carl and said, "Come on, sooner we get done here, sooner we get to go home and clean the dirt off ourselves." Carl smiled and picked himself up off the dirt.

The men wandered the bivouac until they found both Fern and Abram standing around waiting for stuff to do. The two pairs exchanged greetings with one another before Abram gave them their briefing.

"Okay, shit bags, here's today: we run one patrol around the streets on the north side of the town, then we get to go back to the airfield with all the chemical weapons we confiscated. If all goes smoothly, as in no fuckery or shitnanigans, we should be home by 13:30." Abram reported. It may have just been Harvard's imagination, but he was certain even Abram was exhausted from the day before.

Harvard took a sip from his coffee while making eye contact with Fern, prompting the man to nod in gratitude for Harvard's patronage. "Sergeant?" Harvard began, "When are we supposed to get moving?"

Abram looked at his watch, then groaned. "In fifteen. Finish your coffee, grab your weapons. I want you all back here in five." With that, the men disappeared to collect their gear.

It only took Harvard a few minutes to get ready for his patrol, as his rifle was sitting soundly underneath his cot. He placed it on his bed, then strapped on his fully resupplied combat vest, helmet, et cetera. After he was in full kit, he picked up his rifle and returned to the meeting place Abram had designated. Of course, he was the only person who was ready to move, even before the sergeant himself.

In solitude, he simply watched the world go by. He watched the sun creep ever more over the hilltops until Abram arrived, then Carl, then Fern, all late. Regardless, they were present, and thus ready to move.

"Aye! Let's move!" Abram ordered, prompting the men to begin walking towards the northernmost exit of the encampment the American forces had established in the town. Passing through the imaginary gate was almost as surreal as the fighting had been the day previous. Everything was in shambles, the roads were cracked, the houses resembled blocks of swiss cheese from the white washed walls that were now violated by gunfire. Some of the houses had been leveled by explosives.

None of the men said anything, perhaps because the marching was simply a grim reminder to them as to the atrocities they had witnessed just the day before. The machine-guns had ceased, however, and the artillery had fired its last. The town was silent. The only sounds that met Harvard's ears were the sounds of boots on cracked asphalt.

If he was being completely honest, Harvard welcomed the silence. The lack of guns meant that for once, nobody was trying to kill each other. Everything was okay, or at least everything at that moment was okay. Everything at the absolutely very least, felt okay. This was good enough for Harvard.

After about an hour and a half of marching, the men reached the outermost perimeter of the town, where the men simply turned around to walk the path they had just taken. The footfalls of the men still was the only thing to reach Harvard's ears, say for the slight wind that was now to the men's front.

"I'm hungry." Fern said to break the silence.

"You're always hungry." Harvard seemed slightly agitated that his wonderful silence had been broken by such pointless banter.

"Am not." Fern sounded like a fifteen year old rich girl from Harvard's hometown.

"Oh really? You've never gotten a case of the munchies?" Harvard prodded.

"Well, I mean yeah. Everyone who is a part of the 420th infantry division has." Fern giggled.

"Did you just fucking defile my army?" Abram growled.

"Nah man, nah. Chill. It's a running joke with all the weed smokers of the army!" Fern kept giggling.

"Fern?" Carl began.

"Yeah, dude?"

"Shut the fuck up." Carl spat.

"Whoa. Hey did Carl just say fuck?" Harvard asked.

"I believe he just did." Abram replied.

"I didn't even think he could." Fern added.

"I swear all the time." Carl's voice cracked ever so slightly.

"I can't recall one time you've ever said anything close to a bad word." Harvard teased.

"Neither can I." Abram poked Carl with the butt of his rifle as a playful tease. Carl elbowed the sergeant.

With a sigh, Carl spoke, "Look, I try not to, it's just this operation has taken a lot out of me. I'm sure you understand." Carl looked to Harvard as a silent reminder of his duty to Daisy.

"Yeah," Harvard's voice grew somber as the sound of boots filled his ears, "Yeah we do." The men continued their silent march towards the encampment, realizing they had done a sub-par job of their patrol. It didn't matter too much to them, as they just wanted to go home, but the nagging thought was still in the back of Harvard's mind: there was the possibility they missed something.

It was a long while before the men returned back to the heavily fortified headquarters of this operation, but once they returned they found the place exactly how they left it. It was 10:32 when the men returned, which was almost ahead of schedule, meaning the men might be able to take showers sooner.

The men maneuvered through the encampment until they found both First Lieutenant Paul and Second Lieutenant Stern. They exchanged salutes with each other, before Abram reported their findings. "Gentlemen, there is nothing to report in the northern region of the town. I believe the entire town is secure."

Paul smiled a genuinely, while Stern seemed to force one. "Outstanding! Reports are the same from the other teams we dispatched." Paul's focus shifted to Lieutenant Stern. "Alright, send them home. They've done enough for your little campaign."

Second Lieutenant Stern's fiery gaze met Harvard's, and with a sigh gave the order, "Fine. You gentlemen are relieved from your post. Return to Ulysses and freshen up, you all smell like poverty." It was perhaps the nicest thing Stern had ever done for him, which did nothing to thwart Harvard's disdain for the Lieutenant.

"Yes, sir." Abram patted Harvard on the shoulder, prompting the men to began marching away towards a decent place to wait while the convoy was prepared. Harvard wasn't certain where that place would be, but anything was better than being within fifteen feet of Stern.

CHAPTER 13 - BLAKESLEE

His old uniform had been completely discarded; there was no salvaging any piece of it. Harvard had pulled a completely new set from his duffle bag down to the tan tee-shirt he had underneath. The only things he was unable to replace were his boots, which remained as thrashed and dirty as they did back in the little town. Every time he would look down, those service boots would remind him of what he did there—a reminder of the lives he ended, and the lives he saved.

He stepped out of the shower in nothing more than a towel and shower sandals. The showers were empty, say for Harvard and a neatly folded uniform sitting on a bench waiting for him. He got to work, completely drying himself off before slipping on his standard issue underwear and a pair of green boot socks. Then the undershirt, his trousers, tucked the undershirt, then buttoned up his blouse. Finally, he secured his belt.

With a smile, he looked at the all but perfect uniform he was wearing in the mirror. It wasn't ironed, and the insignia hadn't been properly measured on his shoulders, but he still looked presentable. He fancied himself as one of those soldiers who could melt a girl's heart with a passing glance, at least until his eyes met the blood stained boots sitting on the bench next to him. Those were not the boots of a romanticist's soldier, but rather the boots of a soldier who had not only seen the horrors of war, he had also participated in them. Those were his boots, and he would have to live with that fact.

It didn't matter though, he knew he had to wear them for the rest of his deployment, just like how he would have to wear the fresh scars on his body for the rest of his life. He stuck his foot into it's corresponding boot, then zipped up the side, tucked the laces in as well as his trousers to at least make it appear like it was properly bloused. With a sigh, he repeated the process again with his other boot.

That concluded his business in the showers, so he promptly exited and found himself on the airfield. After the conflict in the town, he never thought the sight of Ulysses could bring him so much happiness.

This being the case, he needed to see Ranger if for no other reason than to make sure that he was okay, so he began quickly walking towards the on base hospital. His boots had lost so much tread during the one trip into the town that they no longer sounded the same as they once did on the tarmac. They sounded muted, muffled, generally less pleasant. Perhaps the stains left on the felt exterior was toying with his thoughts, as though the souls of the lives he ended were fighting a new battle within the confines of his psyche.

It was that, or he was simply losing his mind. As he opened the doors of the hospital, he decided to add another purpose to his visit: he was going to see the on base psychologist.

He entered the hospital to find that the receptionist wasn't paying any attention to anything; which was honestly to be expected at this point. He cleared his throat to get his attention, initiating a slow and agitated response from the private first class sitting at the desk. "Can I help you?" He groaned.

"Yeah, I want to see Private First Class Canine Ranger, and see the shrink." Harvard matched the private's tone. The receptionist punched a few keys on his keyboard before looking up to Harvard.

"Ranger can't be seen right now, doctor's orders, and Doctor Blakeslee is on his break so there's not jack shit I can do for you." The private returned to being a useless waste of human potential by picking up a pen and drawing phallic symbols on a piece of paper.

"There's nothing you can do for someone who just invaded a small town? Maybe someone who's worried they might have PTSD and/or depression?" Harvard grit his teeth, comparing this poor usage of military budget to Second Lieutenant Stern.

The private sighed and without taking his eyes off his paper, "Have you tried, I don't know, not being depressed?"

"You're a piece of shit. Ranger is my fucking service dog, he's as much a part of my kit as is my rifle. At least tell me what room he's in so I can take a look through the window in the door." Harvard's palms grew sweaty as his fists grew tighter.

"No can do, asshole." The private drew an arrow to one of the genital drawings and scribbled "Harvard" in nearly illegible handwriting.

"How do you sleep at night knowing you're the reason we have veterans putting bullets in their heads back home?" Harvard asked, bits of fire spewing from his mouth as the words left his lips.

The private sighed and put down his pen, "Thirty milligrams of temazepam." The private looked back up at Harvard, but refused to make eye contact with him, "I'm just doing my job, alright? I was an EOD for a good three months, then I transferred here because I lost my dog to an IED." The private picked up a picture sitting on his desk and held it up to Harvard. In it was a team of four men and a beagle in the desert. Two of the men were in standard kit, while the other two were in bomb suits. In the arms of one of the suited men sat a little beagle. "Stubby, was his name. He was born missing half his tail, so they named him Stubby."

Harvard's heart sank, fully understanding that this man wasn't much different than he was. "I'm so sorry." Harvard muttered.

"Don't be, it wasn't your fault. We all lose something out here, it's just that some of us lose more than others." The private set the picture back down on his desk. "Come back in a few hours, Doc might be back then."

The doors to the hospital opened and an officer walked in, prompting both men to snap to attention and greet the man. It was a major, but he looked far too young for the rank. At a glance, he looked to be only in his late twenties. "Good afternoon, gentlemen." The officer tipped his cover before removing it as a gesture of ease. This man obviously wasn't too interested in the military customs and courtesies.

The private's eyes met Harvard's for the first time, "Well, looks like he's back early." He shifted his attention to Doctor Blakeslee, "Sir, are you able to take a walk in?" The officer spun around and studied Harvard for a brief moment.

"Absolutely! Is this him?" The major casually walked up to Harvard, although stopped at a comfortable pace and a half distance away. This major had his hands in his pockets, cover tucked between his arm and his torso, a surefire sign that the military was not his top priority.

"Yes, sir." The private reported. Major Blakeslee took his right hand out of his pocket and extended it.

"Pleasure to meet you, Harvard. I'm Doctor Eli Blakeslee. We can go to my office, or we can take a walk around the airfield if that seems better for you." Harvard didn't know what to say or do, he had never met an officer that was so easygoing before. He found it interesting that the doctor didn't introduce himself as "Major Eli Blakeslee" and instead opted for his medical profession.

With a pause, Harvard spoke, "Let's go to your office." Blakeslee smiled as Harvard shook his hand. He then gestured down a hallway, and the two men began walking, passing room after room, each a different purpose.

The doctor took a few moments to study his patient, analyzing the way he walked, the number of cuts on his exposed flesh, and the stains on his boots. He concluded that Harvard had been through more than most people did in Birkinistan. "So, is this your first deployment?" Blakeslee asked as an icebreaker, but Harvard simply replied with the standard "Yes, sir," and nothing else. Eventually, the men reached his office.

It was well furnished, a neatly organized desk, a potted plant in the corner, a plush couch placed against the leftmost wall with a metal folding chair sitting across from it. There was a line of blue painter's tape on the floor in the doorway. "Here it is. You've just entered a safe space. Safe from salutes, sirs, screaming, et cetera. Take a seat in that couch over there." Blakeslee gestured to the couch, prompting Harvard to slowly move forward and plant himself securely on it.

Blakeslee sat across from him in the folding chair with a smile on his face. "So, Harvard, what seems to be on your mind?" He asked. He wasn't certain where to begin, as there was so much he wanted to say, but the words wouldn't formulate in his mind.

"I'm not sure where to start, sir."

"Don't call me sir, Harvard. I'm your friend." Blakeslee had a voice like freshly brewed tea, silky, warm, calming. It was as though his voice itself was giving the command "at ease" without Blakeslee saying the words at all. "Let's start with something easy then, how are you sleeping at night?"

He stopped to think for a minute before replying. "As of recently, or throughout my whole deployment?"

Blakeslee set his cover on his lap, "Well, let's start with throughout your whole deployment."

"Well, when I first got here, I don't know, seven or eight months ago, I had a bit of trouble just because I was in an unfamiliar place." He began staring off into space as he spoke, picking one fixed point on the horizon to focus all of his attention on, "But after about a week I was sleeping fine, and I was like that for a good while." His gaze fell slightly, "But it's different now. Most nights I can't sleep more than four hours, and a lot of the time I wake up every hour on the hour. And at least once a week I stare at the bunk above me the entire night."

Blakeslee nodded and listened intently to Harvard speak, "Did anything happen to perhaps trigger that?"

"Yeah, actually." Harvard's fingers traced the couch's seams, "I was out on patrol around Gamarra and we overheard a firefight.

We went to investigate and we found four dead soldiers and one dead Haji." Harvard replayed the sound of gunfire in his mind.

"Were you a part of the conflict in any way?" Blakeslee asked. Harvard simply shook his head. "And that was your first view of fighting, am I right?"

Harvard shifted his gaze to Blakeslee's eyes, "Yeah, that was. I mean I obviously heard gunfire in the valleys before, and I heard stories about the fighting from other men, but I hadn't been there before…" He paused, "I touched the dead Haji by accident… made me puke."

"And how did you sleep that night?" Blakeslee asked.

"I don't think I slept well, but I do believe I got a solid six hours in at least." Blakeslee reached into his pocket and removed a pen and pad of paper.

He started scribbling notes onto it, occasionally looking up to study Harvard for a brief moment before returning to his notes. "Judging by that nice scrape on your left cheek, I can tell that you've seen more conflict. What else is possibly be troubling you?"

Harvard sighed and let his face fall into his palms. "I shot a kid." He mumbled.

"Pardon?"

His eyes met Major Blakeslee's calming coppery irises, "I shot a kid." The words resonated in Blakeslee's ears as the implications of what Harvard just said were made clear. It was evident that the patient wouldn't have simply shot a child for the sake of killing a child; he must've had his reasons.

Blakeslee wrote carefully, "Shot a child," on a line on his pad of paper, "That can certainly mess someone up. You don't strike me as the kind of person to kill someone just to kill them, I'm guessing you had your reasons."

Harvard nodded, "He had a gun to my friend. I just saw the gun and Carl and I didn't know what to do." Tears began to form in Harvard's eyes, "So I pulled the trigger." His voice became more frantic, he shifted uncomfortably in his seat, "And the aid workers were there and there was so much blood and I killed him." Harvard inhaled quickly, "I killed him…"

Blakeslee fumbled slightly with his pen, but regained his composure. "Harvard, I just want you to know that you did the right thing. I know it doesn't change the fact that you killed a child, but if you didn't pull the trigger, your friend would be dead."

"But that's where you're wrong, Doc." Harvard sniffled, "My sergeant figured out that it was just a BB gun." Harvard's gaze fell to his boots, "Does that make me a murderer?"

"Harvard, there's no way you could've known. Regardless of what you think, you did the right thing." Blakeslee recorded Harvard's behavior while he was retelling the events of the bar. "What happened next?"

Harvard slouched in his position, feeling as though the weight of the world was on his shoulders until he was all but crushed by it. "I was taken to Captain Porfiry, where I was interrogated by Paul, Porfiry, and…" Harvard's hands formed fists, "Stern." Harvard shot up and his eyes bored into Blakeslee, "I hate Stern, and Stern hates me."

Blakeslee gave a knowing half smile, "Most people who come in here do. You're certainly not alone in that regard. What did he do to you?" Blakeslee made another subsection of notes titled "Stern".

"He wanted to get me arrested for murder, he did everything in his power to make sure Porfiry thought I was a killer at heart. If it wasn't for Paul, I probably would be in a prison somewhere." He retuned to the omnipresent thousand yard stare, "Stern, of course, wasn't pleased I got off without any repercussions, so he tried to kill me."

"Really?"

"I have no proof, but he convinced Captain Levi to move to the town." Harvard still wouldn't shift his gaze, "He sent me and my friends to that little town in the valley, I don't know its name. I just got back from that hell a few hours ago."

Blakeslee's gaze found Harvard's boots. "And that's where you saw firsthand what war looked like."

"I never want to see it ever again." Harvard said solemnly as his mind returned to the hillside, and the IED on the road, and his best friend screaming in agony. Harvard felt bile rise to his throat, but he pushed it down. The scent of blood flooded his nostrils as he returned to the house with the knife in his hand. Memories that he had blocked out of his mind broke through the wall he put up to defend himself with explosive force. Then as quickly as they appeared, they vanished with the faint sound of a helicopter's engines starting snapping Harvard back to the present.

Blakeslee sighed and stood up to make his way to his desk. Harvard watched as the doctor opened up a filing cabinet and shuffled through some folders occasionally stopping to study one. He eventually found the papers he was looking for, and removed them from their folder, placing them on his desk.

The doctor picked up a pencil and clipboard, then attached the paper he removed. He examined the paper one final time, just to make sure it was the correct one, then returned to Harvard.

"Alright," He began, "Here is a questionnaire to test a little theory of mine. It's quite lengthy, so just be aware of that. You're in no rush though, we have all the time in the world." He extended the clipboard to his patient, which he accepted along with the pencil. "Answer honestly, this is for your own health. There's no sense in lying." Blakeslee gave Harvard the same understanding smile he always wore

"Alright, Doc." He picked up the pencil and read the first question on the painfully white paper. "Do you believe you have Post Traumatic Stress Disorder?" There were three possible answers in bubbles beneath it. "Yes", "No", and "I don't know". Harvard bubbled in the first answer in the list before moving on to the next question.

It was almost mechanical the way Harvard answered each question; simply reading the question, bubbling the most honest answer he could, then moving on. It was a fairly standard test, each question was either A, B, or C, and yet it felt so foreign to him. He wasn't being asked to find "x" or read a passage for comprehension, it was about his own life. Each question seemed to be specifically designed for Harvard's current situation and nobody else's. It was almost degrading to him, yet he pressed forward. His pencil was his weapon and this test was his field of battle.

The ordeal wasn't nearly as intense for Doctor Blakeslee, as he simply watched Harvard mechanically go through the questions to the imaginary cadence in his head. Page after page, he stood by and silently watched, simply listening to the scribbling of pencil on paper. He wasn't idly waiting, he was still studying his patient. He found there was invaluable insight as to what made a person tick when they were left in silence and to their own devices.

Halfway complete with the test, Harvard stopped as he read the question, breaking the cadence in his mind. "Do you have thoughts of suicide?" He was only given two possible answers: "Yes" or "No".

Doctor Blakeslee's words echoed in Harvard's mind, "Answer honestly, this is for your own health. There's no sense in lying." Harvard knew which was the correct answer in the eyes of the Army, and he knew the honest answer that he was supposed to circle. The pencil shook in his hand as he bubbled in his answer.

After that one question, the rest of the questionnaire was quite simple and less invasive, although still incredibly personal. He continued to answer as truthfully as he could for the sake of his health. He trusted the doctor enough to give him some of his innermost thoughts about anything.

Blakeslee still watched him work his way through the last questions, making mental notes of his movements. Once he finished with the test, Blakeslee smiled and extended his hand to take the clipboard from him. "I know it's intrusive, but I trust you answered everything honestly." Harvard nodded almost mechanically. The doctor studied the first few questions answered on the test, then looked up to his patient, "So, this is going to take some time to get finished. I want to see you back here next week, okay?"

"Okay." Harvard murmured in response. The two men lifted themselves out of their seats, and exchanged one last handshake before the doctor walked his patient to the door.

Halfway through the door, Harvard felt the doctor's hand on his shoulder, prompting him to face the man. "We're going to get through this together," Doctor Blakeslee's understanding smile never faded, "I promise."

"Thank you. I appreciate it." Harvard smiled, and he began walking down the hall towards the door to the airfield, passing the receptionist's desk. He left for the airfield, being sure to turn around to give his best facsimile of Blakeslee's understanding smile to the private sitting there. It was returned with a simple wave of his hand.

He wasn't sure how long he had been with the doctor, as it seemed much darker on the airfield, as if it was night, but it was far too warm to be night. He looked around to find that the sky was cloudy, a first for the entire time he was stationed in Birkinistan. The change in skies were welcomed, as it would mean cooler temperatures for the rest of the day.

As he walked, he wasn't certain if Doctor Blakeslee had made any actual progress in helping him. Maybe the first session was simply to try to see what the issues were, if any issues were present in the first place. Still, it was disappointing to say the least, as he probably wouldn't be able to fall asleep that night, or if he did he would simply be plagued by nightmares. That was his life now, and perhaps it would be best to embrace the darkness that clouded his mind. Perhaps.

CHAPTER 14 - NORTON

First Lieutenant Paul and General Norton sat across from each other in the General's office in almost complete silence. On the desk was a quarter of an inch thick manilla folder labeled "Operation Sword of God", an operation that was just ordered by the President of the United States himself.

General Norton sighed, not taking his eyes off the folder. "The orders are in, Paul." He placed his right hand on the opening of the folder, and flicked the papers across his thumb. "Everything is in this folder."

Paul knew what the contents of that folder were before General Norton even told him. "We're assassinating him, aren't we?" He asked apprehensively. The general simply nodded and opened the folder to it's first document, then slid the entire folder across the table to Paul. His assumptions were validated as he read the introduction of the document.

"This has been a long time coming." General Norton took the folder back from Paul, closing it in the process. "Sadly I won't get to rip his testicles off and force feed him them after I anally violate him with a lead pipe, but I guess a bullet to the skull will do just as well." General Norton's eyes fell upon the airfield outside his window.

"Sir, that's disgusting and kind of gay." Paul told his superior, "Regardless, I fully support the president's decision to terminate him." Paul examined the folder sitting on the desk for a little while in an attempt to imagine the strategic genius that must be contained within the papers of this operation.

General Norton, on the other hand, knew exactly what was contained within those papers. "Paul, what if I told you that this wasn't the romanticist's idea of a stealth infiltration involving Seal Team Six or whatever?"

Paul thought about the question for a bit, not understanding that it was simply rhetorical. "Well, I would probably be disappointed." General Norton sighed.

"It's not. We're not just assassinating General Saifullah, we're invading his entire stronghold." Paul flinched.

"We're doing what?"

"You heard me, Lieutenant. We're invading his entire stronghold of Hisn Allah. No house will go unsearched, no street will go unswept, and every Terab in those walls will hear the glory that is my favorite musical instrument: field artillery." General Norton slammed his hand onto his desk, then laughed, causing Paul to join in. "It's going to be more badass than the initial invasion!"

"Yes sir!"

"More exhilarating than Kuwait!"

"Yes sir!"

"More erection inducing than West Point's quarterback!"

"Yes sir! Wait, what?"

"What?"

"What about West Point's quarterback?"

"Fuck, I meant cheer captain." General Norton's eyes fell to the left slightly, before quickly returning his gaze to Paul.

"Oh, gotcha. Anyways, how is this going to be done?" Paul asked his superior, disregarding his slightly homosexual slip ups as simple sleep deprivation. The general opened his laptop on his desk and turned it around for Paul to see a map of Hisn Allah and the surrounding terrain for about fifteen kilometers in each direction. The town itself was quite large in a circular patter, about seven kilometers in diameter. The entire place was surrounded by a wall with guard towers at one kilometer intervals along the wall giving a total of twenty two towers.

General Norton placed his finger on a hilltop about three kilometers from the edge of the town. "Field artillery goes here." He moved his finger to a spot on the east side of the town, "This is the only way in and out of the town. We're not putting anyone here because that's one of the most heavily fortified places." His finger fell upon a section of the wall in a residential section of the town, "Artillery blows a massive hole in the wall here, along with a bunch of houses. Mechanized infantry moves in." General Norton placed his finger on a mosque in the exact center of the town. "General Saifullah knows that it is against the law for us to destroy religious buildings and kill civilians, so he built his palace inside the mosque in the center of town. Anything that flies over it gets shot down, and artillery can't touch it."

Paul scratched the back of his head. "So what do we do about it?" General Norton laughed.

"We breach the fuck out of it. Rangers move in and fuck shit up, kill or capture Saifullah, depending on if he surrenders or not, then we keep killing his men until they surrender or all die."

General Norton closed the laptop. "There's obviously going to be much more, it's just that most of this is in this here folder." He gently tapped the folder with his thumb. "I can't say much else other than you and your company are one hundred percent going to be deployed there."

Paul nodded understandingly, then sighed. He knew that his men would not be too happy with the idea, but it wasn't up to them. They had a job to do. "When does this shit show begin?" He asked.

General Norton glanced at his watch, "Artillery is moving in five minutes, first shells are supposed to drop at 21:00 exactly. Your men, on the other hand, are supposed to be there by 04:30 tomorrow. Let them know what's going on at dinner tonight." General Norton ordered. "God knows they'll need a full belly. You're dismissed, get some chow, shuteye, et cetera."

Paul stood up out of his seat, pushed in his chair, and saluted the General, which was returned with a seated and casual salute. He exited General Norton's office and marched out of the offices onto the airfield. He decided it would be a good idea to return to his CHU to see if he could find Harvard to talk to about the invasion, figuring that he probably had some valuable insight as to what Paul should perhaps do.

It was early in the evening, only 17:06, but the cloudy skies made it feel much later to him. The air itself was much colder too, adding to the late feeling. The sound of gunfire echoed from the valleys around the airfield; the war effort was increasing on both sides. Paul knew this too well, figuring that both sides started to figure out that the conflict itself was nearing an end. There was almost no way that General Saifullah would still be in a position of power by the end of the upcoming operation.

He twisted the handle of the CHU, finding that the lights were on and both Carl and Harvard were present. "Oh, hey guys." He greeted the men, who both didn't respond. Paul checked them to see that Harvard was reading a book in his bunk, and Carl was writing in his journal. "Gentlemen?" He called, prompting Carl to look up from his journal with the same charismatic smile he always wore.

"Good, um, afternoon? I don't know, what time is. Anyways, howdy, Paul." Carl chuckled. Harvard looked up from his book and gave a grunt as his greeting, which was as much acknowledgment as he was willing to push from his soldier.

He sat down on his bunk and sighed, "General Norton has another operation he wants us to be a part of."

"Ah... fuckberries." Harvard groaned as he slammed his book shut with a thud. "Let me guess, we're running patrols in a recently captured city until we get shot in the face and die?"

"No it's way stupider." Paul adjusted his position so that he was laying down on top of the blankets of his bunk, "We're invading Hisn Allah."

There was a brief silence before Carl spoke up, "Didn't we just invade a town? I mean it wasn't too hard, we can do it again." Carl seemed awfully cheerful for someone who was about to be sent into the front lines of perhaps the most dangerous operation in the history of the Birkinistan Campaign.

"Wait, Carl, do you know what Hisn Allah is?" Paul asked.

"Nope." Carl replied.

"Yeah, neither do I." Harvard added.

"It's General Saifullah's stronghold." As Paul's words left his lips, a harsh silence fell over the CHU. Nobody said a word, but Paul could feel the burning glares of both his men on his face. He dared not to return their gaze, as he knew he would only see the faces of absolute hatred staring at him.

Harvard's voice broke the silence, and both Paul and Carl's eardrums, "Are you fucking kidding me?!" In that one exclamation, Harvard's level of volume was equal to Abram's sound off. Neither Paul or Carl had ever heard him so loud or angry ever in the time they had been stationed in Birkinistan.

Paul shook his head slightly, "I really wish I was." He flopped out of bed, boots flat on the linoleum floors. "Believe me, Harvard, I really truly wish I was just joking. Truth of the matter is that the artillery guys are already moving into position and the first shells are dropping at 21:00."

Carl sighed, "At least tell us we get to sleep in. I'm still exhausted from yesterday." He yawned, prompting Paul to yawn as well.

"We need to be at Hisn Allah at 04:30, which means everyone has to be in full kit by 03:00, which means all of us have to be awake by 02:00, which means I have to be awake by 01:30 to get everything ready." Paul groaned and flopped back into his bunk. "I hate my job."

"You're telling us: the assholes who have to be actually shooting at people at oh-four-fucking-thirty." Harvard snarled.

"Harvard, I'm also going to be shooting at people at oh-four-fucking-thirty! Do you think I'm just going to let my company go in without me? Absolutely not, I'm going in too!" Paul spat. The CHU fell silent once more as the men did nothing but stare off into space collectively.

Paul wasn't certain how long they all sat there quietly, but it felt like a long time; it felt like a good thirty minutes or so. Carl climbed out of his bunk and landed on the floor with a muffled thud. "Well, I'm hungry, and it's about 17:30, so I'm going to the DFAC. Get Abram and Fern, we're all eating together as a family one last time." He ordered as he began to walk out the door, but stopped as his hand touched the knob, "One last time." He repeated, then exited the CHU.

Harvard placed the book on the floor, then he too climbed out of his bunk to make his way over to Paul. "Sorry I yelled at you. It's not your fault we're going out there again. Come get dinner, we can get ready for tomorrow's bullshittery." Harvard smiled at Paul.

"Sounds good." Paul replied and graciously accepted Harvard's hand to help him out of his bunk. As the two men walked to the door, it swung open to reveal Second Lieutenant Stern standing there with a manilla folder in his hand.

"Where's my salute, Harvard?" Stern asked, prompting Harvard to snap to attention, and instead of giving a proper salute with a bladed hand, he flipped the bird and allowed his middle finger to touch the tip of his eyebrow as though it were a military standard salute. "Fuck you too, Private."

Paul furrowed his eyebrow and addressed both the men, "Stop acting like children. Stern, what do you want?" The Second Lieutenant held out the manilla folder for Paul.

"This is everything you need to know for Operation Sword of God. I believe it contains an in depth report of what your men need to accomplish tomorrow." Stern realized that Harvard was still holding his "salute". "Order arms, piece of shit." Stern ordered, prompting Harvard to drop his "salute" with an ornery smirk on his face.

Paul took the folder from Stern, and tucked it under his arm. "Thank you, now get out of our way."

"Why?"

"I don't need a reason, I'm higher rank than you." Stern sighed and moved out the men's way, but followed them as they marched to the DFAC. Both Paul and Harvard simply chose to ignore the pestering lieutenant as they walked and talked. Every once in a while the second lieutenant would add in some arbitrary and annoying comment about the subject matter.

Eventually the men reached the DFAC where they broke away from Stern to find the rest of the normal crew sitting at their usual table. Harvard sat down and as his eyes met his lieutenant's, he heard him say, "Hey Harvard, I'll be back with your usual. It's the least I can do for you considering tomorrow."

"Uh… Thank you, sir." Harvard stammered on his words ever so slightly, but gave Paul a gratuitous smile.

It was taco night again, brining back memories of that first night he met Carl weeks ago. A shiver ran down his spine as he remembered the bean projectile nugget flying into his nose.

Although to Harvard's surprise, when he glanced to Carl, he found that his friend hadn't so much as taken a bite of his food yet. It was astounding, Carl's plate still had one chicken taco and one beef taco still in place without so much as a crumb gone. Harvard found the situation almost as troublesome as the first taco night, but for completely different reasons.

"You good, Carl?" Harvard asked, receiving a nod from his friend with the same plastered smile standard on his face. He shifted his gaze to Abram, who wasn't eating an MRE, but instead he had actual food on his plate. Once again, this was troubling.

His gaze fell upon Fern, who kept the consistency of having an absurd amount of on his plate. Three chicken tacos, four beef tacos, a bowl of sweet corn, two bowls of rice, and a large soda.

He further kept up the absurdity by shoveling food into his face at a near inhuman pace, allowing bits of foodstuff to fall onto his uniform. Harvard felt the familiar disgust that he had grown accustom to simply by watching Fern. This display, despite being disgusting, was almost comforting.

"Here you go, Harvard." Paul gently placed a tray with Harvard's taco night usual in front of him; two beef tacos, a bowl of beans, and a box of apple juice. It was the exact same meal he had when he first met Carl all those weeks ago.

Paul sat down with his food, and began saying grace. Harvard decided that he's simply begin eating his tacos instead of waiting for Paul to finish his prayer. He reached down to pick up his beef taco, but the moment his hand touched the tortilla shell, the ground rumbled as a hard thump hit the windows and walls of the DFAC. This thump was followed by another, and another, and then the sirens of Ulysses roared to life. They were under attack.

"You have got to be fucking kidding me." Abram said with a mouthful of food, "Mortars? Really? Goat fuckers can't do math for shit!" As the words left his mouth, a HMMWV outside the DFAC was hit straight on and shrapnel shattered the windows of the DFAC.

"You sure about that, sarge?!" Fern shouted as he flipped his tray over and drew his handgun, prompting the other men to stand up and draw their weapons as well.

"Get to cover, right fucking now!" Paul ordered. The men, without hesitation, ejected from their seats and fell face first onto the ground in an attempt to make themselves as small of targets as they possibly could. With each thunderous bang of mortar strikes, more debris and shrapnel flew across the DFAC. One soldier had been impaled by a flying piece of MRAP.

Harvard peaked slightly to survey the damage only to find that the runway was on fire, as a mortar shell landed on a fuel truck blowing the entire thing apart. There were at least twenty corpses on the runway, all of them missing limbs. This was most certainly not a random attack, this was coordinated, calculated, preplanned.

Then the mortar strike was over just as soon as it began. The last shell dropped on the runway, just as an A-10 flew over and annihilated the mortar crews on the hills surrounding the airfield. Though the explosions stopped, the damage was done. The runway had multiple holes in it that needed to be repaired. Three HMMWVs were destroyed, and thirty one soldiers were either killed or wounded in the attack. Ulysses had turned into just another war torn town, only this time it felt personal.

A few memoryless hours later, Harvard and Carl were sitting in the CHU in complete silence. Harvard read while Carl wrote. Neither of them actually were engaged with what they were doing, they simply were working to take their mind off of the attack on their home base and the inevitable attack on Hisn Allah.

"You know we're going to get them back for this." Carl said to break the silence.

"Yeah." Harvard replied in a hushed tone. The silence returned to the CHU as the men distracted themselves from the world, the war, everything. It was all too much to handle right then, so they chose not to handle it. They chose to pretend that everything was fine simply because that's what they absolutely had to do.

The door to the CHU swung open to reveal Abram in full kit. "Up and at 'em, ladies! General Norton is accelerating the plan! First shells dropped fifteen minutes ago and we're supposed to be kickin' bricks and shootin' shits at oh-hundred!" Abram sounded off, completely deafening the poor soldiers who were trying to distract themselves from their harsh reality.

As ordered, the men moved as quickly as they could to put on their gear and pack their bags. Abram continued his shouting, "Your weapons are already in the truck, along with some rip-its and MREs! Get moving! Pack rain gear!" The men moved even faster, struggling to open zippers and button their blouses. "Come on! My grandma moves faster than you and she's been dead for twenty six years!" Abram screamed directly into Carl's ear.

"Yes sergeant!" Carl cried as he moved even faster to get ready for the invasion. Harvard accelerated his preparations as well to avoid getting smoked by his sergeant, although this did nothing to thwart him.

"You're slower than your mom in bed last night!" Abram screamed into Harvard's ears.

"Good one, sergeant!" Carl smiled.

"Kiss ass!" Harvard chimed in.

"Shut the fuck up, Carl!" Abram sounded off. Eventually the men were ready to move, which acted as an order for Abram to funnel them out of the house at double time pace. Their boots hit the ground at lightning speeds, although all three of the men were almost in perfect step.

The men piled into the back of a truck with the entire platoon, weapons and everything. It was cramped, reminiscent of the cattle cars Hitler would transport the Jews to extermination camps, or the landing crafts that were deployed in Normandy on D-Day.

That's when it hit him, "This is our D-Day." This would be the day that Harvard would remember for the rest of his life, the day that he would tell his children about, the day he would tell his grandchildren about. This was the day that the 159th Infantry Division stormed into Death's castle, looked him in the eye, and shot him in the head. The engine of the truck roared in response, and they began advancing forward into the night.

CHAPTER 15 - HISN ALLAH

"I will shit fury!" It was a random one of the men in the truck who broke the monotony of the road, "And you will drown." Slowly all of the soldiers turned their heads and bodies to face the man who stared into oblivion with wide, unchanging, unfeeling eyes. His face was covered in a thick layer of black grease, or soot, Harvard wasn't certain. His uniform was stained with dirt and perhaps blood, covering the green and white pixel pattern from blouse to trousers. Harvard's eyes found the man's once tan boots, now blackened by the war. This man had seen the darkest parts of the human race, and lived to tell the tale.

Yet Harvard's eyes fell upon this soldier's once again, the yellow swirls of pain within those irises told a different story. This man had seen the darkest parts of the human race, but one could hardly call existing with a broken mind living. Harvard wished he could bring this soldier to Major Blakeslee to help him, but those eyes said that he was too far gone for anyone to be of any help. He feared that this man would not survive the civilian world.

"Alright!" A voice exploded from the front of the truck, but it was too packed for Harvard to get a good look at the source, "Hisn

Allah is only a kilo out! We're dropping you sorry shits off in a section of the city we artilleried the fuck out of. Nothing's left there aside from tent-fucking-city. Your job is to clear the houses along side so that cavalry, armor, convoy, who the fuck knows, can move on through without the camel fuckers blowin' a hole through them and making our day suck more than slut on prom night." A small giggled erupted among the men. "Once you're all done, and hopefully still in one piece, report back to HQ for reassignment. Some of you will get to stick around there, but most of you will be sent back out into the field to capture more territory. Understood?!"

The soldiers replied in perfect unison, "Yes, First Sergeant!" Say for Harvard, who was unaware of the man's rank and position.

The monotony of the road continued, the standard roaring of tires on a cracked asphalt road filled the personnel carrier, invading and caressing the men's ears. Soon enough, however, the sound of the road wasn't the only thing that flooded Harvard's ears, but rather the combined noise of the road and the faint sound of gunfire in the distance. It was almost rhythmic, there was a bump in the road punctuated by a sharp thump, every couple of seconds.

About half an hour went by before the truck arrived at its destination of Tent City, a half mile in radius semicircle of decimated buildings and broken dreams. The truck came to a stop outside of a large tent with a satellite dish sitting on a platform nearby. The men were ordered to disembark, which was a nightmare to do as everyone tried to get out of the tiny opening in the back of the truck at once. Harvard had been trampled by several soldiers, forcing him to the ground, then inevitably kicked out by their boots. With a thump, he hit the dirt with minor scratches on his body, but not harmed in the slightest.

He stood up, collected his belongings, and reported to Abram along with the rest of his squad. The world was still cast in early morning darkness, but everything was illuminated from industrial floodlights and the flames of war in the background. The sounds of conflict were omnipresent, the cracks, bangs, explosions echoed throughout Hisn Allah; a reminder of Harvard's purpose for being there.

Abram finished speaking to a captain about their mission, then maneuvered himself to address Paul. They spoke in hushed tones for a few minutes, before they exchanged salutes. "Let's move! We can't waste any time!" Abram shouted, for a brief moment blocking the sounds of death in the city.

"Yes, Sergeant!" The men replied, then they all marched together out of the safe zone and into the city. As they passed the threshold from Tent City to Hisn Allah, Harvard was almost stunned by the city's beauty. Everything was an ivory white color, say for the buildings that had been either leveled or perforated by machine guns, the roads were at some point pristine, and in front of every house was a raised flower bed dotted with the most beautiful white lilies he had ever laid eyes on.

As the men marched by these gorgeous beds, he felt the uncontrollable urge to pick one, just one. They for whatever reason reminded him of Wystan, as her skin was the same color as those gorgeous flowers. He wanted to give her one and deliver this perfect line, "Now I brought you this flower to show it what a true beauty looks like." He had never even gone on a date with her, but that face, those eyes, that smile; it was everything he wanted. He would find her after this was over and take her somewhere nice.

Then the sound of mortar fire snapped him back to reality. It wasn't at their position, not by at least five hundred meters, but it was enough to remind Harvard of what his job was. The explosions rumbled the ground beneath him, sending pulses of adrenaline through his veins. Still, the men pressed onward.

Eventually the men found themselves at the first house that didn't have an orange "C" painted on its ivory walls. The lilies planted in those beds hadn't been watered in a long while, they were all wilted and weathered. "Ready, Harvard?" Carl asked as he got into position to breach the front door of the house.

Harvard sighed and raised his weapon, "Ready as I'll ever be." With a swift kick, Carl broke the door off it's hinges and the men moved in, clearing the building just as they did back in the little town in the valley. They searched upstairs, downstairs, the pantry, kitchen, even under the beds and found nothing. This house, however, was much higher class than the ones in the town. The furniture matched the exterior aesthetic of white, but also had a gorgeous blue tone to it. "Clear!" Harvard shouted as he completed his search of the upstairs, then the men moved out the the building and into the cityscape once more.

Abram profaned the white wall of the house with a florescent orange "C", before the men pressed forward to the neighboring house. This time Paul decided he wanted to breach the door. "It's not fair that you all get to do proper soldiering, and I have to sit in an office making spreadsheets all day."

Abram shrugged his shoulders, "Yes sir, go right ahead." Paul got into position, placing himself directly in front of the door. He took a deep breath in, then kicked the door with all his might. It didn't even budge. Paul kicked the door again, harder than before, causing the wood to crack and the blue paint to splinter, but the door stayed in tact. One last time, Paul kicked the door, but his foot passed through the wood and his leg got stuck, prompting an eruption of laughter from the men.

Paul twisted himself to face the men and shouted, "Shut up, assholes! This isn't funny! Someone help me out!" Harvard and Fern grabbed onto Paul and on a count of three, tugged on Paul until he was freed from the door. All three of the men fell backwards onto their bottoms as the momentum transferred.

"You good man?" Fern asked, but only received a nod from Paul. The men picked themselves up off the dirt, while Carl used the hole that Paul made in the door to disengage the lock and simply twist the handle open. The men already knew the house was empty, as anyone who was inside would've shot through the door and walls to kill them. Since everyone in the normal crew was still alive, it was safe to assume the house was clear.

Even still, the men thoroughly searched the house, leaving no corner unswept to assure that no American life would be lost. "Clear!" Fern sounded off once the entire house had been checked, then the men piled out of the house to move on to the next.

Harvard was still struck by the city's beauty, even though he had been vandalizing it with his attempts to clear a path for the convoy to push through. The city was just too gorgeous to be left alone. Harvard simply wished he could spare it from the inevitable destruction it would face at the hands of American forces. He knew there was no way he could.

The next house, Harvard decided he would take point and breach the door. With both Carl and Abram standing on his right and left respectively, Harvard kicked the door as hard as he could, forcing it to fly open. There were two men who were unarmed as they weren't expecting to be attacked. Quickly Harvard reacted to the sight of two enemy soldiers with a sharp "On your knees!" He wasn't about to kill someone if he didn't have to, but he was certain he would as the men dove away as a smoke grenade filled the room with a thick gray fog. "Hold your fire, there might be civilians!" Paul ordered, "Pop smoke."

"Popping smoke!" Harvard shouted as he removed a cylindrical grenade from his vest, removed the pin and tossed it into the house. He heard it clank against the floor, then a small crack emitted from the grenade as a cloud of white smoke filled the room. "Go! Go! Go!" Harvard ordered as both he and Carl entered the building at the same time with Fern, Abram and Paul following in the rear.

The men used the smoke to conceal their positions, knowing full well that the enemy had the same advantage as they did. Everything was silent for a little while, until the men heard footsteps from above them. The faint pitter-patter of boots on a wooden floor above them was enough to send Harvard's mind into a frenzy.

He quickly glanced to Paul, who gave the hand motion to proceed up the stairs. Harvard replied with a salute, then quietly moved up the stairs, alone. His boots creaked on the wooden steps, but his vision was cleared of the smoke. Everything was deafeningly silent, say for the thumping of Harvard's heart.

He was right in the doorway to the bedroom of the house, having to bite the inside of his cheek just so he didn't scream from the nerves. His breaths shortened, becoming sharp and at irregular intervals. In front of him was the white wooden door, behind that was the enemy. He had several options, he could slowly open the door and pray the enemy wasn't right there waiting for him, he could kick the door down and shoot anything that moved, or perhaps he could simply shoot through the door and hope he hit something.

But he waited too long to make his decision. He heard voices on the other end of the door, and as he raised his weapon to make his move, the silence was replaced with the sound of explosions. Instantly several holes were punched in the wooden door and dry wall as bullets flew straight at him. He hit the floor, face in the wooden flooring. All he could do was wait until the barrage of bullets ceased, but it didn't. It seemed as if the hostile men took turns reloading and firing to maximize the amount of ordinance flying through the wall ant potentially into his face.

Then it all stopped in an instant. Harvard dared not to move from his prone position, but silently readied his rifle for the inevitable. He knew the Birkinistani soldiers would push through that door to check and make sure they had killed him, or at least wounded him to the point he could be apprehended. He refused to let himself be killed by these beasts—the same beasts that shot his dog.

He almost didn't notice it, the slow methodical opening of the door. In fact, he didn't notice the door slowly opening at all, just the black leather boot that had somehow poked its way through the cracked open door. He still played dead on the floor, waiting for the enemy soldiers to fully reveal themselves to him.

The door had opened just enough for him to see his enemy's face, he heard the soldier whisper something in his native language to his compatriot. He received a whisper back, then the soldier addressed Harvard's still body.

In an instant, everything turned red as blood sprayed out from the enemy's torso, and skull, and limbs. He open fired on both of the enemy soldiers, not really aiming, just shooting. It wasn't a need to kill the enemy, it was a need for survival. He emptied his entire magazine, all twenty rounds went into the two men, some even received the same bullet as it penetrated both soldiers. As the twentieth round flew from the muzzle, the breach locked open signaling that the rifle was empty.

Someone was screaming. He knew it wasn't the enemy soldiers, they had been torn to pieces. It was him. He was screaming, but he wasn't hurt, he had been incredibly lucky. Harvard silenced himself, having to put his own hand over his mouth to stop his subconscious mind from whaling uncontrollably. He wan't certain why he was screaming, he just knew he had to stop.

Once he regained his composure, he picked himself up onto his feet, ejected his spent magazine, replaced it, then quietly crept into the bedroom to assess the damage. The scenery itself was terrible, almost everything had been destroyed, the furniture had been splintered beyond recognition, the once white walls were grayed from the paint being torn off from rifle fire. Covering the floors was a thick layer feathers and fluff from the bedding.

The white feathers were contrasted by the bright, almost glowing red liquid that covered the walls and floors. The corpses of the enemy soldiers had been mutilated beyond recognition. Severed limbs dotted the floors, the faces of both the soldiers had been completely removed, exposing a grotesque display of mangled flesh and bone. One of the men still had an eye left in tact, at least a little bit. Bone fragments cut it open, letting liquid ooze out as though it were a ketchup packet that had been torn on one end.

Harvard stepped off with his left foot, weapon ready to shoot anything he deemed a threat to his security. His footfalls were muffled by the feathers and soft debris on the floor, but he could still feel the squelching of his boot in viscera. He was surprised he didn't vomit then and there to add to the mess, but he didn't seem disgusted in the slightest. He was simply horrified that he had to do what he did in the first place, and that he would have to live with it for the rest of his life.

The room was clear, but before Harvard could leave to alert the others, his eyes fell upon the one single eye mangled corpse of the enemy soldier. It was the exact same color as the boy's from Gamarra. That was the moment Harvard felt disgusted, and in an attempt to keep himself from hurling on the floor, he left the room as quickly as he possibly could. "Clear!" He gagged, and immediately heard footsteps coming up the stairs.

Paul's eyes met Harvard's. "You good, man?" He simply pointed behind him at the mess in the bedroom. Paul gagged as he surveyed the damage done to the enemy men. "Jesus H. Christ!" He exclaimed before grabbing Harvard's shoulder and escorting him down the stairs and into the living room.

"All good?" Carl asked.

"He really made a mess up there. I counted what I can only assume are the remains of two goat gropers, but Harvard turned them into tomato paste." Paul sighed, "It's disgusting." Paul and Harvard's met eyes once more, both men staring into each other to see how bad the war had affected them. He found that Paul had developed bags under his eyes from sleep deprivation, and Paul had found the same with him. But Harvard had something he didn't, something that Paul never wanted to have: the thousand yard stare. Even in that tiny moment of time, he was staring into the void as though it could stare back.

Abram grunted, "Let's move. There are at least thirty more houses we need to clear before the convoy can push forward, and I really want to go to bed." His voice was quieter than normal, Harvard could tell that he also was suffering the effects of sleep deprivation.

Harvard felt a hand on his shoulder, "Hey, cheer up man." It was Carl, "You're still alive, ain't ya? Think about what happened later, we have a job to do." He told him as everyone slowly marched out of the room. Harvard knew Carl was right, he really needed to focus on the task at hand. Morale was critical, especially since he hadn't gotten a good night's rest in a long time.

Harvard's eyes fell upon Carl's, "You're right." He said, "Lead the way." The men marched their way to the next house that needed to be cleared, and Carl decided he would breach the door.

"Excuse me, do you have a moment to talk about our lord and savior?" Carl began, then shot the lock off the door with his M16, "Our lord and savior, *Freedom?!*" He shouted as the other men pushed into the building to clear it. Each soldier took his own room, sweeping and clearing, then shouting "Clear" to alert the others. Everything was clear, so the men simply moved on to the next house, repeating the process several times without Carl's idiotic one liners.

The men swept another house, then another, and another, and repeated the same mechanical searching process at least nineteen times before the first of the convoy appeared on the roads only a few hundred meters behind them.

Harvard felt an elbow in his side, and turned his head to see Abram standing next to him. "Front of the convoy, it's the redhead. You should wave to her." Taking point on the convoy was an M3 Bradley from the cavalry scouts, specifically Wystan's Bradley.

"What? Why?" Harvard asked.

"You like her don't you? Don't tell me you don't." Abram teased.

"I'm not waving."

"Do it."

"No, sergeant."

"Come on!"

"Not happening."

"No balls."

"Excuse me?"

"No balls!" Abram repeated, then turned to face the other men. "Harvard's got no balls!"

"No balls!" Fern shouted, then Paul followed, and even Carl pointed and said those two words. With a sigh, Harvard turned to face Wystan's M3 Bradley and waved. After a few moments, the 25 millimeter gun pointed directly upward, then the turret tilted side to side a few degrees quickly, followed by a short honk from the machine's horn.

Harvard laughed, "I think that was supposed to be a wave back." He smiled, not realizing that the gun was repositioning slowly to aim at the rooftops surrounding the convoy. Then everything erupted into gunfire, enemy infantry had them surrounded. The men scattered instinctively to find cover while the cavalry fired at the enemy soldiers above them.

Paul ordered the men to engage the enemy, which prompted Harvard to point their weapons in the general area of where the enemy was. If he was being honest, Harvard really had no idea where the enemy soldiers were shooting from. He only knew that someone was shooting at him from the rooftops above, and they were probably going to get torn to shreds by the gorgeous redhead with the tank.

The rattling of machine-gun fire could be felt even the couple hundred meters that he was from the convoy. Everything around them was exploding, buildings started to crumble from the ordinance that was being pumped into it.

At some point during the fighting, Paul gave an order of some sort, but Harvard couldn't recall what he said. All he knew was that he was moving quickly while the cracking of bullets followed behind him very closely.

They were behind cover, he didn't remember how they got there, he didn't remember a thing. All he knew was that somehow he and his friends were facing the enemy directly and he was ordered to shoot them. He poked his head from out of cover to spot an enemy, but the sudden impact of bullets in front of him forced him back. "Paul! I don't have a shot!" Harvard shouted.

Paul raised his rifle to rest it on a roadblock in front of him and fired blindly in the general direction of the enemy. "Must I do everything around here?!" Paul shouted, then fully revealed himself to aim at an enemy.

In the time it took Harvard to blink, Paul was on his back staring up at the black sky. "Fuck!" Harvard couldn't believe what was right in front of him, "Paul's been hit!" He reported to his squad mates.

"Fuck!" Abram sounded off, right as a well placed artillery strike leveled the buildings that the enemy combatants were shooting from. The cavalry cleaned up the mess with extremely accurate 25 millimeter fire. There was only one house that still was somewhat standing, and that had no cover on it whatsoever. It was very safe to assume that all the enemy combatants had been neutralized.

The men rushed to Paul's position, where they found that he was covered in a thick layer of dirt and soot. Paul stared blankly into the night sky, although the slow rise and fall of his chest indicated that he was in fact still alive. "Paul?" Harvard felt tears welling up in his eyes.

Paul reached up with his hand as if there was something above him. "Am I going to die, Harvard?" Paul asked.

Harvard grabbed Paul's hand, "No, no you're going to be fine. I promise." A corpsman slid on his knees beside them with his first aid kit ready.

"Oh Harvard, I see Him." Paul was smiling with blood dripping down his face. Harvard wiped away a tear with his free hand.

"See who, sir?" He asked. The corpsman let out a giggle, which absolutely infuriated Harvard.

"I see the Lord!" Paul exclaimed, then he turned his head to the corpsman, "Doc, just let me go. I'm so close to Him now."

"Don't you fucking dare." Harvard snapped to the corpsman, who was obviously trying his best not to laugh.

"I see Jesus, Harvard. And he's b…" Paul stuttered, "B…"

"Beautiful?" Harvard asked.

"He's… black." Paul sounded horrified, then quickly addressed the corpsman, "Please don't let me die, Doc! I think I'm the first man who doesn't want to go to heaven!" The corpsman simply shook his head then addressed Harvard and the rest of the men.

"Alright," The corpsman began, "So your lieutenant is fine, the sniper shot him right in the body armor. He's got a broken rib, but he'll be alright. As for the delirium, he hit himself on the back of the head. No permanent brain damage as far as I can tell, he's just totally fucked right now. I'm going to call for medevac, but there's nothing seriously wrong with him." The corpsman picked him up and held him like a damsel after she had been rescued in a fairytale. "One last thing, he knows I'm black, right?"

Harvard shrugged, relieved that his friend would be fine, "I have no idea, Doc. Thanks." The corpsman nodded, and began the march all the way back to Tent City for medevac. Something in his heart told Harvard that this would be the last time he'd see Paul.

"Let's move." Abram ordered, prompting Harvard and the rest of the men to return to their task of searching the houses. As his foot hit the ground, he heard the unmistakable bang of a launcher type weapon, and the sickening sound of a High-Explosive-Anti-Tank round hitting a metal vehicle.

Harvard turned to face the direction the projectile came from to find a Birkinistani soldier running quickly away from the soldiers on the road. He took aim, then fired one single shot directly in front of his adversary. The bullet hit the soldier in the flank, passing through all his vital organs and killed him near instantly.

Then came the damage report. Slowly he turned around to assess what the enemy soldier had hit, and what he found forced Harvard to his knees. In the exact front of the convoy was a mangled and destroyed M3 Bradley. Wystan was dead.

CHAPTER 16 - CARL

It had been sixteen hours later and the sky was still dark. Clouds of black smoke covered the skies above, allowing only a few rays of sunlight to pierce through and leave streaks of light falling onto the ground. The world smelled of ash and misery. The beautiful town that was Hisn Allah had been reduced to rubble and embers, say for the mosque in the center that remained untouched. That mosque was just out of range from artillery fire, and had too much anti-air defenses to risk a bombing run.

It seemed almost impenetrable, as General Saifullah had ordered all but a couple squads to defend his compound. Friendly forces simply couldn't move in to take it, but the Birkinistani General couldn't escape; he was surrounded. The mosque had three armor teams, two cavalry regiments, seven different sniper teams, a ranger unit, and almost the entirety of the 159th Infantry Division set up so that nothing could leave without being shot to pieces. This stalemate was anything but a cease fire, however. Soldiers on each side of the firing line took potshots at each other simply to try to whittle down the enemy forces.

Harvard had found himself sitting on top of a standing building that had a decent enough vantage point for his purposes: nap time. He couldn't even remember the last time he got a full night's sleep, and the fact that he didn't even get to rest since the invasion of the little town in the valley wasn't helping in the slightest. He wasn't the only one either, as the others in his squad decided it would be best to sleep on that rooftop as well. Nobody was shooting in their direction, and the enemy patrols wouldn't get past the blockade placed about 500 meters from their location. It was the perfect setup for a bit of much needed shuteye.

To their dismay, however, the men wouldn't get their much deserved rest, as their new platoon commander arrived to greet them. "Wake up you sorry shits!" He shouted as loud as he could. His voice almost made Harvard cry.

"Please for the love of God not let it be him." He whimpered as his head lifted off his backpack to stare Second Lieutenant Stern directly in the eyes. "God fucking damn it."

Lieutenant Stern groaned as he too realized who he was in charge of. "It ain't a picnic for me either, Harvard." The relaxing soldiers picked themselves up from off the floor and each saluted their new platoon commander. The Lieutenant dropped his backpack and removed a can of Rip-It energy drink, "I have one for each of you."

Harvard was utterly confused. It seemed as though Stern had some sort of compassion in him, or at least enough to know how to get his men moving. Carl's voice broke the question that was on everyone's mind, "Is Paul going to be okay?"

Stern sighed as he finished unpacking the Rip-Its, each of which he placed neatly in a two by two square. "He's fine, or at least we're expecting him to be. He might be out of service for a while, I'm afraid." He picked up one of the cans, "Carl, catch." With a light toss, the can was flung about fifteen feet from Stern's hands to Carl's. He eagerly cracked the can open and took a sip, marveling in the fizz from the soda. Fern was next, receiving his can in the same manner.

"Hey Stern, do we have intel on how in fuck's shit we're gonna smoke General Fucks-a-lot?" Abram asked as he caught his can with one hand, and adjusted his helmet in the other.

"I have no idea. I heard talk that they're going to bomb the mosque with a Harvest Hawk, then MARSOC parachutes in while the armor kills everyone. Rangers go in with MARSOC and kill or capture General Saifullah." Lieutenant Stern explained before he picked up the last can of Rip-It and tossed it to Harvard. He cracked open the can, and took a sip, astonished that the liquid inside was actually cold.

"Well," Abram began, "What do us eleven-bang-bangs do in the meantime?" Abram had reached into his vest pouch to remove a bottle of 600 milligram ibuprofen tablets.

Stern then watched him in horror as Abram popped three of the pills into his mouth, then drank the rest of the Rip-It to wash it down in under fifteen seconds. Abram then crushed the can in his hand, and tossed it off the edge of the building. "I uh…" Second Lieutenant Stern turned to Carl, "Does he normally do that?"

"Yeah that's Abram for ya."

"Right." Second Lieutenant Stern redressed the men as a unit, "I guess we're just supposed to watch. Levi hasn't given me any orders other than reassigning me to replace Paul for the time being. I think the war is over, at least for us." Second Lieutenant Stern surveyed the ruined cityscape.

Harvard did as well, allowing the cool, fizzy bliss of caffeine to slowly take effect. Bit by bit the smoke cleared from the skies revealing a brilliant blue that had long since been forgotten. He imagined that it was the boy from Gamarra, the people from the little town in the valley, and the people he shot in the house all staring down at him to tell him that they forgave him for what he did. He imagined that it was Wystan smiling at him to keep moving forward. He wasn't about to disappoint her.

That was until the first mortar was fired from inside the mosque's walls landed directly into NATO forces' positions. To Harvard's surprise, there wasn't an explosion when the shells hit. In fact there wasn't anything other than the thump of an object striking the ground at high velocity. "Well that was weird." Harvard shrugged as he took a sip of his drink.

"Heh. Fuckin' hajis don't know how to use arty." Abram chuckled.

The world still seemed peaceful despite the occasional gunshot echoing through the air, and the ever-present sounds of conflict, and the screaming. He heard screaming. Harvard looked around quickly to find that he wasn't the only one who heard the blood curdling screams of tortured men. They were louder than any sound off, and they were coming from right below him.

At once, Harvard knew what had happened. He quickly threw off his backpack and frantically searched for his gas mask because he knew what would happen to him if he didn't find it. "Harvard?" Carl asked. He ignored him, hoping that his friend would figure out what he was doing fast enough to be spared. "Harvard? What are you doing?"

He needed not to reply to Carl, as the radio attached to Second Lieutenant Stern's vest did all the talking. "All callsigns, this is Crossroads, be advised: the blue water contingency is in effect."

"Oh fuck." Abram was shivering as he quickly dropped his backpack and equipped his mask.

"Blue water contingency? What the fuck is that?" Fern asked.

"They deployed their nerve gas. Everyone, masks on now!" Stern ordered. He didn't need to tell anyone twice. Quickly everyone's M40 gas masks were strapped tightly to their faces and secured.

The screaming had ceased, Harvard knew the men were dead. It only took a minute to kill a person with sarin, a fact that was made extremely clear to anyone who got stationed in Birkinistan. He was safe though, however he wasn't sure how much of friendly forces remained in Hisn Allah. He turned to address Stern, who was on the radio trying to figure out the casualties and their orders.

Harvard, along with the rest of the men, simply took positions around the rooftop with weapons ready. They had established a decent perimeter, as they had a view of everything around them. Harvard wished they didn't, however, as he had the unfortunate task of defending the side that had six convulsing soldiers right in his line of sight. They all looked to be in excruciating pain, and there was nothing he could do for them.

Abram was right next to him, he too was looking directly at the soldiers who were dying on the ground. "There's two left alive." He told Harvard. With a sigh he added, "You take the one on the left, I got the one on the right. Get him in the head, we don't need them to suffer anymore."

Harvard's heart sank with his command. "Sergeant, are you suggesting we kill these men?" He choked as the words left his mouth.

"They're going to die, I don't want them to suffer. Now do the right thing, Harvard, that's an order." He did as he was told, aligning the sights of his rifle so that he could hit the man directly in the head. On a count from three, both triggers were pulled at the same time, and both men were dead before the sound even hit their ears. Harvard wanted to puke, but he couldn't because he'd drown in his own vomit. To him, that was a worse way to die than by the nerve agent floating around him. It was colorless, odorless, tasteless, but one drop would be enough to kill a man.

The men still stood guard, trying not to let anxiety get the best of them. Nobody was shooting at them, they had their masks on, they were safe. "Gentlemen, the brass wants you all to carry out the contingency as planned. There's nothing for us here anymore, they want everyone looking for survivors and wounded. Everyone's going home, complete tactical retreat." Stern explained.

"Wait, we're not going after Saifullah?" Harvard asked.

"No, we're not. Get moving, maybe you'll be a hero. God knows you need to make up for Gamarra." Stern grumbled as he marched away, leaving the rest of the men to carry out his orders. He did have two other squads to take care of as the new platoon commander. Still, as the second lieutenant walked away, Harvard thought it would be so easy to put a bullet in the back of his head. Accidents did happen.

But before he could even decide if he wanted to shoot Stern or not, the rest of the men began moving down the rubble which acted almost like a second staircase. He followed close behind until they could reassemble into a more evenly spaced group as they searched for survivors.

Just as they had many times before, the men marched house to house clearing them to find anyone who was still alive inside. In the first house, they found six corpses; a dead man and woman, as well as four dead children. Each of them looked to have been killed by the gas, as their eyes were glazed over and foam was still stuck to their mouths. Some of them had defecated and urinated, probably without their consent.

Abram lead the men to the next house, which was empty say for an unexploded mortar shell that had punched a hole straight through the roof, upper floor, and had stuck itself into a kitchen countertop. It had obviously the mechanism that delivered the chemicals into the vicinity. "Everything within a 200 meter radius of this thing is dead by now. There's no point in searching these houses." Harvard announced.

"You're right. Let's get…" Abram trailed off, listening to the sound of an engine, perhaps. It kept getting closer, being identified as a motorcycle of some sort. As the sound grew ever closer, it was obvious that it was a motorcycle, although it was unclear if there was more than one.

Fern was listening attentively, standing right next to Carl. "What kind of motorcycle do you think it is?" He asked, of course not seeming to understand the danger that they were in. Nobody answered his question, but simply moved into positions where they wouldn't be seen. More than likely, it was a few Birkinistani soldiers looking for survivors to slaughter.

Harvard nervously flicked the safety of his rifle on and off, ready to shoot anything that threatened him or his friends. "Probably a Haji Davidson." Carl replied.

"Shut the fuck up, Carl." Both Harvard and Abram growled in unison. The motorcycles drove past the house that the men had taken refuge in slowly, but in a few minutes they disappeared into the depths of Hisn Allah. The men breathed a sigh of relief, and quietly moved out of the house and began walking in a straight line out of the affected area of the mortar strike. The gas was likely clear by this point, but none of the men were willing to risk that. They had seen the bodies so they knew what it looked like; they didn't need to know what it felt like. Harvard simply tried to block the images from his mind, not wanting to see the faces of the damned any longer.

Truth be told, Harvard didn't even want to see the faces of the living anymore. Everyone had seen too much; too much of what no man should ever have to see. He himself had seen too much of the darkness to ever truly see the light again. Harvard just wanted to go home. There was nothing that could make him want to stay in the hell that was Birkinistan anymore.

The men reached a spot that, theoretically, the sarin had hit less severe. More people should have survived in this section of the city than where the mortar hit. "Do we know it was sarin?" Harvard asked.

"Do I look like a chemical expert to you? Maybe you should take your mask off. Find out." Abram replied, probably with a look of utter disgust underneath his gas mask.

"I was just wondering." Harvard muttered. The men continued marching, as there was nothing to do other than push forward. The houses on either sides of the streets had been completely destroyed, leaving nothing but rubble in their place. It seemed as though it was a long, continuous, uninterrupted pile of debris that passed alongside them, which overflowed onto the streets. It was so surreal, Harvard was awestruck at what just one day of conflict could do to a beautiful city such as Hisn Allah.

He counted the cadence in his head to take his mind off of the dead people who once lived here. It wasn't their fault that they were born in Birkinistan under an oppressive regime, nor was it their fault that America decided to invade during their lifetime, and it certainly wasn't their fault that General Saifullah ordered their homes to be destroyed by a chemical weapon to cover his escape. Nothing was their fault; it was all just luck.

Luck. That was funny to him. As an atheist, Harvard didn't really believe that there was some higher power forcing the world to his will, but rather that everything was based on probability. There were 7.2 billion people alive in the world at the time, and of those 7.2 billion people each person had a one in 300 million chance that the sperm that entered the egg would be that specific sperm. Of each person that was born, every life had an equal chance to be placed anywhere in the world, and with so many people being born at once, anyone could have been anywhere. The numbers said that these people would be born in Birkinistan. The numbers said they would live in Hisn Allah during the Birkinistan Campaign. The numbers then decided that these people would die in Hisn Allah.

Abram snapped Harvard out of his thoughts with a simple raise of his left hand. The entire squad halted at once, weapons ready. "Never mind. I thought I heard something." He announced, then took one step forward. This would be the last thing he did before a bullet struck him straight in the chest, knocking Abram flat on his butt. "Fuck! Get to cover!" He shouted as he picked himself up off the ground and the men scattered.

Harvard looked directly at Abram, bewildered that he was fighting, let alone still alive. The men fired blindly into a cloud of smoke, obviously where the enemy forces were concealing themselves. Abram's armor plate was exposed from the bullet slamming into his vest, tearing the nylon and pouches to reveal the cold black steel. Once the mystery of Abram's magic chest was gone, Harvard began returning fire at the enemy.

Nobody was certain where the enemy was at all, however they knew they were there as green tracers flew through a pillar of smoke and incredibly close to their positions. Harvard wondered if the enemy had somehow obtained thermal optics and was using them to see through the smog. It was possible that General Saifullah had killed all the grunts in the city and had to operate solely on his special forces. These thoughts made Harvard shiver.

Suddenly, there was an unexpected cease fire that went on for a few moments before anyone shifted positions. Abram tried to move to some better cover, but he only fell on his chest as his legs gave out. "God damn it, I can't..." He coughed under his mask, "I need a doctor."

"Fern, Carl!" Harvard called, "Get Abram to HQ. I'll flank them to cover your escape and rendezvous with you later."

"Roger that, Harv." Fern began helping Abram to his feet.

"No. I'm not leaving." Carl said. "No one dies alone."

Harvard turned to face his friend. Under that mask, he knew that he was smiling that same, ever present grin. "You sure?" He asked.

"Positive."

"Heh," Abram chuckled, "That damn Texan. Make me proud, boys." With that he and Carl retreated about two hundred meters in a full on sprint, not even stopping to catch their breath.

Running in all that gear and with the M40 mask on was a near impossible task, but the adrenaline from the fighting must have been what was pushing them forward.

Carl and Harvard locked eyes, and in perfect synchronization ejected their magazines to see how much they had left. To both their surprise, their weapons were adequately armed, so they reinserted their magazines as a unit. The men then pushed towards a crack in the rubble, where they could move along to the adjacent street to flank the enemy. "You ready to do this, Carl?" Harvard asked, voice trembling.

Carl only nodded, knowing full well that the enemy they were facing was anything but a standard infantryman. In their hearts, they knew this was something else. They knew that someone was going to die today, and they could only hope and pray it wasn't them.

The men moved on through the adjacent street at a jogging pace to keep their strength. The nagging thought was in their mind that perhaps Fern and Abram had been killed and the hostiles were looking for them now. Maybe they were too late and there was nobody to flank, and their friends were dead, or hurt, or captured. Maybe the enemy had ripped the masks off them and they were dying on the ground from the nerve agent.

"Harvard!" Carl shouted as he stopped, but he kept running, then he was on the floor. His head was pounding, but he wasn't severely injured. He heard the sounds of close gunfire, followed by what could only be the sickening crunch of bones snapping from a fall. He looked to his right to find the bleeding corpse of a man in a black chemical suit and Israeli gas mask. Carl rushed over to his friend, "Ah man, they got you right in the helmet."

"I am so damn lucky. Had I been running any faster, I'd be dead." Harvard giggled at the incredibly probability, nerves, adrenaline, he didn't even know. He was just thankful to be alive.

Carl reached down with an open hand, "Come on. One last dance, old friend?"

Harvard grabbed ahold and said, "Yeah. Why not?" The moment he was back on his feet, they began their sprint once more, being even more wary of hostiles in the area. The thoughts returned to Harvard's head, wondering if the enemy he was hit by had just shot Abram or Fern and was looking for them next, or if he was detached to find him and Carl. He could hear his heart pounding in his ears, which wasn't helping the stress headache that was forming.

A green tracer cracked past Harvard's head and slammed into the road just a few meters behind him, prompting both of them to seek immediate cover. Harvard searched for the enemy while Carl laid down suppressive fire. The enemy kept firing at Carl's position, each shot landing ever closer to his friend. They took defensive positions; Harvard hid behind a building while Carl used a concrete roadblock to keep the bullets off him.

Then Harvard found him. He was about six hundred yards away, but he could hit him. He was sitting on top of a roof, his black uniform contrasting the white wash walls of the city. Harvard took aim, inhaled a half breath, then squeezed the trigger.

Through his scope he watched part of the walls explode into dust and stone, but no red mist or any indication of a hit. Harvard realigned his reticle to take another shot, but the hostile turned around and open fired on his position. The air cracked as the bullets zipped past, forcing him to retreat back behind the building.

His heart was racing, increasing with every crack and bang from the rifles in the street.

Then it appeared that Carl was drawing this man's fire once more, so Harvard took the opportunity to acquire his target. It seemed as though the world hated him at that very moment, because the instant he stuck his head out from cover, the enemy soldier spotted him and fired a single shot in his direction. The bullet slammed into the wall and sprayed Harvard's face with shrapnel and debris, cutting his face and painting his glasses with dust.

While Harvard hid behind the building wiping his glasses down, he heard a distinct sound: silence. The shooting had ceased completely, not like a lull in the firefight, but absolute zero. Harvard wasn't about to let that stop him, he popped out of cover to scan for the target, and realigned his crosshairs on his prey. The man turned his head and spotted the American hiding in the city, prompting him to duck down the moment the trigger was pulled. He got back up and began sprinting away.

Harvard fired at his enemy one final time, before the man disappeared into the rooftops. He turned to address Carl, when his heart sank in his chest. "No." He muttered, holding back tears. Harvard sprinted faster than he ever could to his friend, who was bleeding on the ground with a freshly punched hole in his chest. Assessing the damage, Carl had been hit in the upper chest and was bleeding heavily. If Harvard's knowledge of human anatomy was right, Carl was shot right where the internal jugular vein was. "Carl, you're going to be okay." Harvard told him, more for himself rather than his friend.

Carl wasn't screaming at all, simply wheezing and groaning occasionally. Harvard knew by this time that the sarin would no longer be a threat, so he ripped Carl's mask off as quickly as he could, followed by his own. "It's going to be fine, Harvard." Carl told him. He couldn't hold back his tears anymore.

"I'm supposed to tell you that!" he cried, "Because you are going to be fine! I promise!" He dropped his M14 and started rummaging through his vest to find a packet of QuikClot. Carl made a noise, almost like a giggle, but Harvard wasn't sure.

Their eyes met, as the words, "Stop making promises you can't keep." escaped his lips. It was followed by a smile, although Carl's teeth were red with blood. Harvard found a packet and tore it open with his teeth and began packing the wound with the coagulant.

"I won't let you die." He kept repeating to himself all while Carl wheezed in his arms.

Carl's gloved hand reached into his fatigues to retrieve his dog tags. He looked up at Harvard and said, "I need you to keep these for me. A little something to remember me by." He coughed.

"Fuck no man, you're going to need those."

"Harvard, it's okay. I did my best." Harvard tore open another packet and began packing the wound some more. He thought that he might actually be able to save Carl, then they could all go back to life on Ulysses like it was — shenanigans in Gamarra just like the old days.

"You remember your duty with the letter to Daisy, right?" He asked. Harvard felt a tear drip off his face and land on Carl's, washing away some of the blood and dirt. Despite his efforts, the bleeding hadn't slowed at all, and he was out of QuikClot.

"You're going to tell her everything yourself, Carl." He began tearing open simple gauze packets to pack the wound, but this too did little to stop Carl's hemorrhaging.

"I need you to tell her I love her for me." Harvard shook his head.

"Carl you're going to tell her that yourself. Then you two are going to get engaged and have a beautiful wedding and have a family and live happily forever." Harvard's tears were streaming down his face as more blood flowed out from the open wound in like a river.

"You and I both know that can't happen."

"Carl…" He whimpered, doing nothing to stop the tears at this point.

"Don't forget me, Harvard. You're the best friend I've ever had." He made one final effort to save him by stuffing more gauze into the wound.

"I promise, Carl." He knew he was too late.

"Give her flowers for me." And he was gone. Carl stopped responding, stopped breathing, stopped living. His eyes stared blankly into oblivion. He looked so peaceful, almost like he was daydreaming. Even in death, Carl still had that innocent smile on his face, like he knew that everything was going to be alright.

CHAPTER 17 - HARVARD

The HH-60 Blackhawk touched down on the landing pad on Ulysses Airfield to unload the wounded and corpses. Harvard had been lucky enough to receive the right to an evacuation after he had been separated from his surviving squad mates. He wondered if they were okay as nobody had heard from the soldiers at least while he was in the air.

Still seated, Harvard watched two crewmen carry Carl's body bag out of the helicopter and delicately lay him down with countless others. He would be shipped back to the United States on the first flight out in a wooden box with an American flag draped over it. He would never get to see Daisy again, and she would never get to see him again.

He watched the black bag sit motionless as tears started to well up in his eyes. All he could do was wish that Carl would unzip the bag and exclaim something along the lines of "I'm not dead, assholes!" Then Harvard would run up to him and give his friend a massive hug.

Thinking about it, Harvard never hugged Carl at all, or called him his best friend. Almost everything he said to the man was an insult, or he teased him, or sent him off to do something stupid for his own amusement. There was so much unfinished business with Carl, so much stuff that Harvard wished he could do now but will never be able to do. Carl was gone, and Harvard just had to move on an accept that fact — he knew this but simply couldn't. "That damn Texan." he whispered to himself.

The pain in his chest was so much greater than anything he'd ever felt, the pain of losing the one and only person who ever believed in him. Perhaps in death, Carl meant even more to him than he realized back when he was alive. He would go so far as to say he loved Carl, not in the way of romance, but rather how an older sibling loved his younger brother. Carl was that to him, if nothing else — his brother.

A crewman's voice snapped Harvard back to reality, "Dude, we gotta unload you. This helo is going back for another medevac. Get on out." Harvard slowly unbuckled his harness, and collected himself. He was dizzy, nauseated, and had a pounding headache from the enemy sniper who shot his helmet. At an excruciatingly leisurely pace, he walked out of the helicopter and onto the airfield. Everyone was moving as quickly as possible, the hospital had several tents set up outside to address the overflow of wounded men from the sarin attack in Hisn Allah.

He didn't know what to do at that point, his commander and dog were in the hospital, his sergeant and surviving squad mate were missing, and his platoon commander hadn't given him any orders. On all fronts, Harvard was on his own.

With nothing else to do, he decided to wander the airfield just as he did many times before back when everyone was still around. He thought maybe he'd go obtain a HMMWV to drive to Gamarra to have a drink with his friends just like old times, then remembered they were all gone. He decided to head to the DFAC to get some food, but when he glanced in its direction he found it had been converted into another command post. Ulysses Airfield wasn't what it used to be. Nothing was what it used to be.

He kept wandering, hoping he could find someone in his chain of command who could reassign him to a place where he could work and take his mind off of what was happening. He didn't like having to be alone with his thoughts, being forced to replay the events of Carl's death over and over again in his mind. Then he had an epiphany, "I could have saved him."

There wasn't any way to know with certainty if he could have prevent Carl's death. All he knew was that he missed, and because he missed the enemy wasn't dead. Because he missed, the enemy soldier shot Carl and killed him. The enemy soldier was still alive somewhere out in Hisn Allah, Harvard knew it. He knew he could never have Carl back, but he could have revenge. He gave himself the new task of killing the man who killed Carl.

"What would I need?" He asked himself. He realized that he left his rifle and gear back in the town to carry Carl faster, so he would need to resupply on everything. The only thing he still had on him was his M9 service pistol and a single fifteen round magazine. This was hardly enough to hunt down the man who killed Carl.

He decided to take a trip to the armory where he would resupply on anything he could get his hands on, preferably an M14 just like the one he used before, although at this point he would be happy with an M16A2 or even an M249 SAW. It didn't matter,

Harvard needed to avenge his brother, and he was willing to go to the end of the world to do so.

He began marching towards the armory, continuing to make a list of everything he would need. As it was a long walk to Hisn Allah from Ulysses Airfield, he would need transportation. With an HMMWV, it would take about two hours to arrive, which was plenty of time to go over the strategies in his head. He decided that the HMMWV would be the best way to get to the city from Ulysses. He would also need night vision goggles in order to see in the darkness that would inevitably shroud the city.

His thoughts were interrupted by a hand on his shoulder, "Hey, Harvard. I heard about Carl. I'm so very sorry for your loss." It was Major Blakeslee, he had that same sympathetic smile on his face. The moment their eyes met, Harvard's bearing broke and he started to cry uncontrollably.

"He killed him, Doc! He killed Carl! He's fucking dead!" Harvard whaled, nearly collapsing onto the floor, but luckily Major Blakeslee caught him and held him upright. He simply allowed Harvard to cry in his arms, doing his best to comfort the soldier in his time of need. Once Harvard had calmed down a bit, he positioned him so that his hands were still on the Private First Class's shoulders.

Major Blakeslee sighed and spoke softly, "I know. It's alright to be sad, y'know. It's what you're supposed to do." The doctor patted Harvard's shoulder with his left hand, then brought his arms back to his sides. "Carl would want you to mourn him because he would want you to be healthy."

Harvard removed his bloody glove before wiping the tears away from his eyes. "I'm going to kill him." Harvard muttered.

"Pardon?"

"I'm going to kill the son of a fuck who killed Carl!" He shouted. Doctor Blakeslee cocked his head as he processed the words that left his mouth.

"You're going to do, what?" He almost couldn't believe that Harvard, after everything he had been through, after everything that had happened to him physically and mentally, would be willing to go back into the line of fire to kill a man.

"I don't need your permission, just your understanding." Harvard scoffed as he began walking towards the armory.

Quickly, Doctor Blakeslee put his arm up to block Harvard from walking any further to obtain the materiel for his self assigned operation. "Harvard, wait just one moment. You can't do that." The Doctor repositioned himself to stare the private directly in the eyes.

Harvard scowled, "Like I said, I don't need your permission."

"No, I mean you can't even go to the armory anymore. You have new orders." Doctor Blakeslee reached into his pocket and removed a sealed white envelope and handed it to Harvard.

The infuriated soldier stuffed the envelope into his pocket. "I don't have time for this, I need to avenge Carl before that God damned camel fucker escapes!" Harvard pushed right past Doctor Blakeslee.

"You've been discharged!" The Doctor shouted at the top of his lungs, prompting the private to stop completely. Those words hit him like a wall of bricks, making his knees shake, his eyes welled up with tears once more. "I'm sorry, Harvard. I had no choice." Doctor Blakeslee put his hand on Harvard's shoulder. "It's a medical discharge, not dishonorable. I had to make the call based off of your test results. I diagnosed you with Post Traumatic Stress Disorder which has made you unfit for continued service."

Harvard sniffled, "Medically discharged?" He repeated the words to himself over and over again in his mind. It was a horrible thing to think about, that everything he had done in his entire career had destroyed his mind to the point that he couldn't serve anymore. The enemy never so much as touched him, and yet they still were able to take him out of service permanently.

"I'm so sorry. I mean that with all I got." Doctor Blakeslee's voice returned to its soft and understanding tone. The two men stood in silence as the rest of the airfield frantically worked to address the catastrophe in Hisn Allah.

Harvard parted his lips to speak, but the words simply wouldn't leave his mouth. The silence continued for a while, although he had no idea how long it was. "Where are Abram and Fern?" He finally asked.

Doctor Blakeslee smiled, "You'll be happy to hear that they returned to HQ in Tent City unharmed. Abram is expected to make a full recovery in a few days. He's just dehydrated."

"Dumbass…" Harvard's gaze shifted into oblivion. "And Paul? How's he?" He managed to ask.

"He's getting better. He'll be up and out of there in just a few more days. He'll be flying out to Torii Station in Okinawa when he's fit for it, given the circumstances surrounding his reassignment. He wishes he could say goodbye to you, but when he's on leave he promised to stop by your house to say hello." Blakeslee smiled. Harvard knew that probably wouldn't happen. It was unlikely that he'd see Paul ever again.

"And Ranger? Will I see him again?"

"Once he's done healing here, he'll be sent back to the states. There was no way anyone was going to keep him from you." The tears started dripping down Harvard's face again, falling in little raindrops and splattering on the tarmac. "You're on the first flight out. The plane's not leaving until you're on it. I'm making sure of it."

Harvard realized that he'd be flying home in the same plane that Carl's dead body was in. He found it fitting that they would both go home together. They served together, fought together, suffered together, but they couldn't die together. At the very least, they would step foot back on American soil together.

Doctor Blakeslee slapped Harvard on the shoulder lightly, "Go take a shower, change into a clean set of ACUs, then pack up your CHU." Harvard sighed.

"Yes, sir." Harvard began walking away, but stopped. "Thank you, Doctor. For everything."

"Just doing my job." The two soldiers parted ways, Harvard heading for his CHU, and Doctor Blakeslee heading for the wounded men.

After a bit of walking, he arrived at his CHU. Everything was still in place, everyone's stuff was scattered about on their beds and floors. He decided it would be best to grab a new set of ACUs before he took a shower. He searched through his belongings to find a clean set, then tucked it under his arm to move towards the showers.

About fifteen minutes later, Harvard found himself outside on the steps of his CHU in a fresh and clean set of ACUs. All the blood and dirt on his face and body had been washed away. Once again the only part of his uniform that he couldn't replace was his boots, which stayed stained and battered from his service. He decided that when he got back to the states, he would buy himself a new set of boots to replace these old ones.

He twisted the handle of his CHU one final time, then stepped foot on the linoleum floors. Harvard made his way to his bunk, where he began packing his things. He loaded everything into his duffle bag, his book, his extra gear, anything he could possibly take home with him. The entire time he packed, his mind flashed back to all the memories he would have of this place. This containerized housing unit was, in every respect, his house; the house he had lived in for the past nine months. Even with all the sleepless nights, it was still hard for him to say goodbye to it.

He sat on his bunk one last time, imagining that he was watching Carl sit on the floor scribbling in his journal with Ranger at his feet, while Paul was reading a book on his bunk. That was the way things were supposed to be, not like how they were now. Then and there, everything was still. The CHU was empty, say for Carl and Paul's scattered belongings.

Harvard decided it was time to go, so he picked himself up along with his duffle bag and began walking out of the CHU, but something out of the corner of his eye stopped him. He turned his head to find Carl's journal sitting on the floor in a clearing of discarded belongings. It seemed to be calling his name, requesting to be taken with him.

He would oblige this journal. He turned around and slowly walked to the black leather journal sitting on the floor. With a trembling hand, he picked it up, and clutched it to his chest. His thumb felt the tops of the pages, knowing that tucked between two of them was the makeshift envelope that contained Carl's letter to Daisy.

The clicking of the door behind him signified the last time Harvard would be in CHUville. He marched forward towards the airfield, all the while letting his mind wander. Carl's final words replayed in his head, "Give her flowers for me."

Harvard knew exactly what kind of flowers he would give Daisy — the white lilies he saw in the flower beds of Hisn Allah. Even with everything that happened in that city, they were the most gorgeous flowers he had ever seen. "Those lilies..." His voice was silk, "Those lilies for Daisy... Those lilies from Carl..." His words gave him the smallest and only bit of closure he could find at that moment.

Harvard found the group of people who were boarding the C-130 that would fly them to Dulles International Airport in Washington D.C. It would be a nonstop flight that would take about 22 hours to complete, but once the plane landed, Harvard would find himself on American soil for the first time in a long time. It had been so long that Harvard didn't even remember what America smelled like.

There were probably around fifty men waiting for the C-130 to arrive, along with fourteen coffins that had American flags draped over them. Each coffin had a tag attached to them with the identification of who's body was inside it. Harvard made it a point to stand directly next to the one marked "Darling, Carl." He knew that if it was him in that box, Carl wouldn't leave his side. He dropped his duffle bag to the floor to get more comfortable while he waited. Harvard decided it was his solemn duty to be Carl's guard, as his friend deserved that much. His friend deserved respect from those who were still alive.

Harvard felt his heels click together as his the toes of his boots were pointed apart at a 45 degree angle. Then his hands formed fists as his thumbs aligned with the seams of his trousers.

His gaze focused straight forward, his baring at maximum. He was at the position of attention.

Then Harvard's boots ordered him to preform a left face, his heels clicking together with the command as his entire body faced the coffin his friend slept in. A single tear dripped down his cheek as he slowly brought his right hand up across his gig line and his middle finger to the tip of his right eyebrow. A solemn salute, for a solemn hero.

One of the soldiers took notice of Harvard's salute, prompting him to drop his bag and go to the position of attention. He too faced the deceased, and saluted. Another soldier was inspired to do the same, then another, and soon enough the entire group of soldiers waiting for the C-130 to carry them out of Birkinistan was standing at attention and saluting the fourteen corpses in the flag draped coffins.

The display almost brought Harvard to tears, as everyone held the salute. Nobody even moved, nobody flinched, nobody said a word. The noises of the airfield were muffled and muted by the respect that each soldier here gave to the deceased. Everything was silent.

Everything was silent until someone began singing. "Day is done." It began. "Gone the sun." It was to the tune of taps. A single female soldier in the rear ends of the group still held the salute as she sang.

"From the lake, from the hills, from the sky;" She continued, although another voice had joined in on the singing. They were the lyrics to "Taps" written by Horace Lorenzo Trim. "All is well, safely rest, God is nigh." Harvard felt more tears drip from his eyes down his cheeks.

"Fading light, dims the sight." More soldiers had joined in on the singing, at least five voices were heard, "And the star gems the sky, gleaming bright. From afar, drawing nigh, falls the night." There were ten distinct voices singing then.

"Thanks and praise, for our days, 'neath the sun, 'neath the stars, 'neath the sky; as we go, this we know, God is nigh." Almost half the soldiers were singing Taps.

"Sun has set, shadows come, time has fled, scouts must go to their beds. Always true to the promise they made." The sound of a C-130 was audible at this point as it neared its final approach to Ulysses Airfield. This didn't stop the final verse from being sang by every soldier in that group, Harvard included.

All together, the soldiers sang the last three lines, "While the light fades from sight, and the stars gleaming rays softly send, to thy hands we our souls, Lord, commend."

At the conclusion of those words, a sergeant in the group called the command, "Order, arms!" Prompting all the soldiers to drop their salutes in unison. "Detail, face!" The sergeant called, the soldiers pivoted 90 degrees to the right to face the runway once again where they watched the C-130 land.

Only ten minutes of waiting passed before the soldiers were allowed to enter the plane that would fly them out of Birkinistan. Still, none of the soldiers moved until a few crewmen were sent to retrieve the coffins. In an act of pure respect, the soldiers formed a single file line behind the flag draped boxes, still at attention. It was a solemn march to honor the fallen, all the while little drops of emotion dripped from Harvard's eyes and splashed upon the tarmac.

Eventually the men broke formation and each sat individually in the plane on either side facing inward towards the coffins. Harvard still clutched Carl's journal tightly to his chest as he didn't want the inevitable turbulence to rip it away from him. He was deciding whether or not he would give the entire journal to Daisy, or just the letter and the lilies. Harvard did want to keep it, not to read, but rather as something to always remember his friend by.

He opened the journal to the page where the letter was tucked in. Thankfully on the makeshift envelope, he found Daisy's address. She lived in Texas, specifically Arlington, which wasn't a surprise. The trip would be of zero concern to Harvard, as he knew Carl would do the same for him.

The four turboprop engines of the C-130 spun to life, causing an eruption of applause from the soldiers in the cabin. They were all going home, all fourteen of the deceased, and all fifty of the living. Everyone aboard that plane had been relieved of their duty as a soldier, some forever, some just for a while. Some of them were crying tears of joy, some simply tilted their covers over their eyes so they could fall asleep. Everyone got to say they were going home.

Harvard's eyes fell upon the red white and blue that had been carefully draped over Carl's coffin. He had fulfilled his duty as a soldier to defend his country at any cost, even at the cost of his own life, with dignity and solemnity. That was Carl's purpose in this world; Harvard suspected that he knew that from the moment he stepped foot into the desert. With his duty fulfilled, Carl could sleep in peace, now and forever.

EPILOGUE - DAISY

My Dearest Carl,

Seventeen nights ago, a chaplain appeared at my doorstep to deliver the news of your passing. To say I was devastated would be understatement. I don't think I went a single night without crying into my pillow, screaming God's name at the wind for taking you from me. My sweet, darling Carl, ripped away for nothing. Then your friend found his way to my home, introducing himself as Private First Class Reginald Harvard—your best friend. The moment our eyes met, he broke down into a mess of tears and apologies.

I invited him inside, as it was raining, and we sat in my living room for the longest time. He was dressed in the same dress uniform that the chaplain was in, his oxfords shining brighter than what I thought our future would look like. And, truth be told my love, I thought our future would be pretty bright.

He had your journal with him, and he said that he wanted to keep it, but if I wanted it that he would give it to me. I let him keep it, your thoughts are private and I shall respect that. This being said, he did give me that letter you wrote me about why you did it. It was beautiful, just as everything you write is.

I still have your book of poems. The one that you wrote all those years ago to ask me to be your girlfriend. I still read them, even more than usual when you left for Birkinistan, and certainly I don't plan on ever stopping now that you're gone. I love you too much to stop.

Back to your friend, he kept saying he was sorry and I asked him why, it's not like he killed you. He told me that he was sorry because he missed the man who shot you, and then he broke down completely. I have never seen anyone so heartbroken before, and I myself am broken beyond all recognition.

He said the flowers came from you, those gorgeous white lilies. He told me that these were the same flowers that you died among in that city. Every time I look at them I can feel you with me, almost as if your soul is bound to them, and in the coming weeks when these flowers wilt I shall know you are departing to that next stage of existence. One day I shall join you in the eternal bliss.

God I miss you Carl. I miss you so much. There's nothing I wouldn't do to have you by my side again. I miss your voice, your smile, your laugh… you. But I won't give in to the temptations to join you in that ethereal beyond. I know you wouldn't want me to. So for now I shall mourn you, and when the day comes, I'll live the life that we always dreamed of. Just me, and you, living forever in my heart and mind.

Yours now and always,
Daisy Burke

ABOUT THE AUTHOR

Jakob Becker—at the time of this book's publication—is a 17 year old high school senior living in Encinitas, California. He's been studying military science and psychology on his own time for almost 5 years at this point. He spent a year in the Civil Air Patrol, USAF Auxiliary and served as the cadet commander for his school's JROTC unit. He's been writing short stories for himself and Speech and Debate for 10 years, although he considers this to be his best work. 30%* of all profits from Lilies for Daisy will be donated to the Wounded Warriors Project, while the rest will be placed in a fund for medical school. Jakob hopes to use this fund to complete a doctorate program to become a psychiatrist and work with veterans who suffer from PTSD and depression.

*Subject to change without notice depending on financial status, valid through date of publication to December 1st, 2023.

ACKNOWLEDGEMENTS

Lily, I am going to admit this right now, I used the majority of my time in your class to write this. I'm sure you already knew that though. That said, I'm not certain this book would be half as good as it is without the techniques and the whatnot I learned in Speech and Debate (outside of class, of course). This story couldn't exist without my time on the team because I actually got the inspiration for it during a round. For that, you have my eternal gratitude. Thank you so much for putting up with me and my shenanigans.

Mom and Dad, thank you so much for all the support you've given me through this project—both emotionally and financially. I don't think there's any way I can ever repay you (mainly because writers don't make jack shit these days), but I hope that this is enough. I hope I made you proud. I love you guys, and I can't wait to do it all again with novel number two (hopefully with money in my pocket this time).

Mr. Ross, there's no way I'd leave out my creative writing teacher from this. Thank you for letting me use your class to perfect the first few drafts of this project. You and the other students helped turn this piece of crap into a slightly less smelly piece of crap. I sincerely miss that hour and a half of my day spent with all of you. So, while I move on to the next part of my life, I'll leave you this as a little parting gift—a token of my appreciation for keeping me sane.

Alex, I don't think I've ever met anyone quite as loyal and caring as you are. Here's a big thank you for all that you've done for me and this project. The support and responsibilities you took on have alleviated much of the stress and fear that I had walking into this. Speaking of responsibilities, it appears I am still alive so a posthumous publication won't be necessary haha. In all seriousness, I can't thank you enough for your support.

Olivia, none of this would exist without you. It all started with a simple text: "If you don't [write a book] I'll be sad and won't send you memes." To protect all of meme-kind, I accepted your challenge. So, here it is a whole two years later. I hope it's as good as I told you it would be. I'd like to sincerely thank you for all the ideas you threw my way—whether they were jokes or serious suggestions—because they added a sort of spice to the story that I could never have come up with alone. Above all else, thank you for turning a pissed off little boy into who I am today: someone I'm proud to be. I don't think I can ever repay you, but you shall forever have my gratitude. Perhaps this is a start, perhaps not. In any case, this is for you, and there's no one else I'd rather give my book to. Thank you for everything. Cheers.

Thank you.

www.ingramcontent.com/pod-product-compliance
Lightning Source LLC
Chambersburg PA
CBHW020551020726

47494CB00006B/2015